Mischief in Macon:

Mischief in Macon:

A Grain of Salt in the Pepper Shaker

Sadie Allran Broome

Tampa, Florida

This book is a work of fiction. The names, characters and events in this book are the products of the author's imagination or are used fictitiously. Any similarity to real persons living or dead is coincidental and not intended by the author.

The content associated with this book is the sole work and responsibility of the author. Gatekeeper Press had no involvement in the generation of this content.

Mischief in Macon: A Grain of Salt in the Pepper Shaker

Published by Gatekeeper Press
7853 Gunn Hwy., Suite 209
Tampa, FL 33626
www.GatekeeperPress.com

Copyright © 2024 by Sadie Allran Broome

All rights reserved. Neither this book, nor any parts within it may be sold or reproduced in any form or by any electronic or mechanical means, including information storage and retrieval systems, without permission in writing from the author. The only exception is by a reviewer, who may quote short excerpts in a review.

ISBN (paperback): 9781662953668
eISBN: 9781662953675
Library of Congress Control Number:

Contents

Acknowledgments	vii
Introduction	ix
The Rug Was Pulled Out From Under Me	1
Leaving Cherryville	10
Tenants on the Uprising	13
School Daze	19
Can You Mix Without a Mixer?	25
The Scout Promise	32
Fire, Theft, Drowning, and Feet Don't Fail Me Now	37
Proms and Proposals	42
The Haunting	50
Let's Be Thankful	57
Christmas Gifts	63
The Joys of Being Mom	70
Woody and Professional Learning	77
The Barrel Cabins	83
The Cherry Blossom Festival	88
Colder Than a Witch's Tit	92
The Magic Kids	99

Is Golf Really a Gentleman's Sport?	106
The Rabbit is Rich	114
Life Can Be a Beach	122
There Goes a Meatball	128
Epilogue 2024	133
Meet the Author	135

Acknowledgments

This work of fiction could not have been written without the patience of my husband, Dennis, who contributed his time, and the encouragement and editing of my daughter, Stephanie, and granddaughter, Abigail Sadie.

The inspiration for the work was our great mischievous and lifelong friends, Barry and Julie, Bill and Valerie, Betty and Eli, Nathan, Albert, Mitch, Jeff, Carl, and Dr. Dorothy Hutley. It greatly enriches your life to have such amazing friends to continue to travel through life's journeys with.

I must acknowledge my sister-in-law, Teresa Broome, who worked on edits throughout the entire process. This was quite a tiresome task, and she never complained. She believed in me!

Mischief in Macon: A Grain of Salt in the Pepper Shaker is dedicated to the memory of Dr. Dorothy Hutley and Albert Taylor, JD.

Introduction

Back in 1981, a teacher's husband decided to go back to school to become an attorney. He moved his little family from the small town of Cherryville, North Carolina, to Macon, GA, so that he could attend Mercer Law School. The husband and wife embarked on an adventure where they made lifelong friends and had numerous mischievous adventures while being far away from home and the life they knew before. They were in culture shock but enjoyed the wild ride. It is the story of love, loyalty, friendship, perseverance, and joy.

The Rug Was Pulled Out From Under Me

Cherryville, North Carolina, was like Mayberry in *The Andy Griffith Show*, with a very small population and not even a courthouse like Mayberry! Everybody knows everybody and from my home place you can walk downtown, and also, we have our steamy scandals like Peyton Place. I lived there all my life until the rug was pulled out from under me.

Cherryville. It is a simple, sleepy little town of less than five thousand people. I come from a family of four. Mom, Dad, my brother, and I lived right in the center of Cherryville within walking distance to town. I grew up knowing most of the people there and have always prided my southern self on forming lots of lasting relationships; relationships that led to my not receiving traffic tickets when I should have, relationships that had the community calling my dad about my antics rather than reporting me to the police, and most importantly relationships that taught me how to love and be loved and how to grab life and live it fully.

Cherryville meant everything to me. Most kids see their senior year in high school as a wonderful time of life with merriment and hope of what is to come. *Not Me.* All I could do was feel a sense of dread. The thought of leaving the halls of Cherryville High School, my teachers, and my friends and of not being a Cherryville Ironman made me feel physically ill. What is an Ironman, you ask? The Ironman is the Cherryville High School Mascot. Annie Mae, me, is a girl person. But I was absolutely an Ironman, a Cherryville High School Ironman through and through. I am sure you think that I am exaggerating about leaving high school making me physically ill, but I can assure you that I am not. I carried on so much, fearing that life as I knew it was ending, that I made myself sick and missed my own senior awards day. In the fall I would only be a few miles away at Gardner Webb University, but I still thought my life was forever changing and that it could not be any better than high school. I loved my best friends dearly. We (The Group) all rode to school together, hung out at non-school times, and had a lot of *shady* adventures. Oh, well that is another book.

Disclaimer: *Before I go further you must understand something about this narrative. My story is from things I have seen, heard, implied, or made up because I thought someone told me. Often flat-out rumor may become a fact in my narrative. I cannot say this strongly enough. I am not researching anything for this story. If you want to know if it's true, try the internet. It is kind of like my narrative, part fact, part rumor, and part total fabrication, and you can never be sure which is which.*

So, to help you understand my life in Cherryville, I am giving you a snippet of our Cherryville world, I'll share just one little story. Halloween is HUGE in Cherryville. I grew up on Elm Street. The culturally literate will understand the implication: Yes, we have always and continue to be, *The Nightmare on Elm Street* with hundreds of trick-or-treaters traveling the sidewalks collecting candy treasures while marveling at the amazing decorations and costumes, some of which are cute and some scary. Each house chooses a different theme and we try to keep themes secret if possible until Halloween.

This Halloween, The Group leaped into my car. I have always been a lousy driver. I tailgate and have no sense of direction. I would always drive to the house of one of the friends and they would take over the driving. My dad gave me his former car which was exceedingly cool, a 1968 Chevelle, lovingly named Pudge. We wore various stages of Halloween costumes and were armed with a load of beer and a trunk full of eggs that we planned to throw later on. It was a tradition to get into some egg-throwing wars with our Elm Street neighbors. This was a Halloween sideline to trick or treating. We teenagers thought we were a little old to go out trick or treating for candy. We would go to the various neighborhoods in town and egg each other. This is the "trick" part of "trick or treat." We drove Pudge down into the lithium mine near Cherryville. *Yes, didn't you go to hang out and drink beer at your local lithium mine out in the country?* We had just settled in to drinking and discussing what the rest of the night might entail when one of the boys and I decided we needed some alone time (just visualize whatever you want, but really, I have to admit it was just kissing). While we were down in a ditch kissing and such, we heard a car coming. He jumped out of the ditch and attempted to stop what he thought was my car full of friends pranking us—oops it was the *police, or as we would say, Poe Leece*. They had the rest of The Group exit the car, and the police quickly confiscated the beer and asked to see in Pudge's trunk. They wanted to know about the eggs, and Louise, one of the girlfriends in The Group, said that we were planning a big breakfast. That did not go over well, and our eggs were confiscated too. After the police left and we piled back into the car, you can imagine the state we were in with no beer and no eggs. It was a quieter than usual Halloween for us that year.

After reading that little tidbit, you can see how even with a less-than-stellar egg-throwing Halloween, we kids in our small town had so much fun. Louise, Linda, Jean, Blanche, and I rode to and from school every day of high school and then included our various boyfriends and friends that were boys on the weekends; often ending up at the lithium mine. I am sure now that you can see why I did not want to leave Cherryville.

I met my husband Paul on the job. I was a teacher of students with disabilities, and he was the school social worker. He thought I had a cute behind and asked me out. I already had a date for that weekend, but I did not want to miss the opportunity to go out with the cool social worker who was a swim coach with a huge afro. I had a code that I never broke a date. I told Paul that I already had a date for that weekend but asked if I could come and cook for him the next weekend. He seemed a little taken aback from that offer from someone he had just met but readily agreed. I went to his apartment and cooked Annie Mae steaks. *As a first-year teacher I had very little money so these were breakfast steaks. Here is my recipe: I put A1 on the steaks and cut onion rings and put on top. I put them in a tin foil packet. I thinly sliced potatoes, put butter and onions on those and wrapped them in foil packets. I baked both at 350 for about 10 minutes. I added a salad, bread and voila—first date meal.*

Because I was in an apartment on a first date with a man that I barely knew, I began to have extreme anxiety and had to run into the bedroom and call Jean, a member of The Group. Fear grew that I was here in an apartment and did not know Paul's intentions. Jean assured me that I had plenty of charm and sass and that I could really run fast, so I would be fine. I have to interject here that on this first date, Paul, not only showed me magic, but he also literally showed me magic tricks; some were like pulling things out of a hat, a magic wand that shot out fire and some were card tricks that became important in my teaching life later on. It turned out to be a great first date.

He was great with Tina Dawn, my daughter, from a prior marriage. This one is hard to explain, but when he proposed, my dad, who I loved dearly, had a massive heart attack. No lie. He had open heart surgery and was in ICU for days. My mom and I were camped out in ICU sleeping on couches and Paul brought Tina Dawn by each day and kept her with him in his apartment at night. I knew then that he was a "keeper" You can really tell the character of a person by how well they stand up during a crisis.

We were married within a year of that first date and lived just down the street from my parents on Elm Street. The first place that my dad went after his heart attack was to give me away at our wedding. In addition to being an effective social worker, Paul was a natural-born actor. He was in numerous plays at our little theater down the street and auditioned for a play entitled *All American*. During the audition process, he met Leonard Goldberg. Leonard was married to Mary, and they had three children, Margaret, Alise, and Neal. They became our lifelong friends. The Goldbergs lived next door to a family who became our lifelong friends also. Every Friday night, we wound up at the Goldberg house along with an assorted menagerie of friends partied, laughed and all carried on into the night while I was usually asleep on the couch after telling a few tall tales and drinking a couple of gin martinis.

We built new relationships within the community. Paul and I used the local Odell's Grocery for deli items and groceries and bought gas at Seller's and at Johnny Reynolds. We frequented those so much, the owners were like personal friends. We also had an account at Ferguson Hardware. The joke was that Paul would come home and say that the nice Mr. Ferguson gave him a knife. Sure he did. Not. But that was a standard joke. Paul has always had fun gifting himself with little things he "needs." Paul will spend money on things he wants whether the money is readily available or not.

Mary Goldberg decided to try Odell's Grocery since we bragged about it so much. When she arrived at the cash register to pay, she was aghast. The "girlie magazines" were right there at checkout beside the candy. She pitched a fit and said that those "girlie magazines" like Hustler and Playboy should not be right there where little children were buying candy, and needless to say she did not become a patron of Odell's.

One evening, Paul came home from work and said that he would like to go back to school. I held my breath, praying (an odd prayer but a prayer nevertheless) that he was not going to say that he had gotten the call to be a preacher. Thankfully, he had decided that he wanted to go to law school. He began the process of filling out applications. He was accepted at Ole Miss, Mercer in Macon, Georgia, and Louisville in Kentucky. We were so excited.

Mom and Dad traveled with us to Ole Miss. Things did not go so well. We could not find any apartments to rent listed in the newspaper. We found out that the apartment owners did not want to rent to blacks and so did not advertise. We were astounded. Then I went for an interview at a mental health facility. The boss was still fighting the Civil War all over again in his mind and thought Mississippi should secede from the Union. Paul and I were literally gape-jawed. The best thing we found in Mississippi were these excellent catfish at the restaurant in our hotel. We grabbed my parents and made a quick exit from that state.

Our next adventure was to Mercer University in Macon, Georgia. The university was beautiful and a staff member there knew of an apartment we could rent on Vineville Avenue that seemed perfect. I went for my interview at the Department for Exceptional Children, in the local school system. My whole family went with me to the interview. My potential employers thought my family was so cute to come with little Annie Mae and said that my rotund and burly dad looked like Berle Ives who was Big Daddy in the movie *Cat on a Hot Tin Roof* and the voice of the snowman in Frozen. The interview went well and I was hired to teach behaviorally challenged students at a local elementary school. We were set. Mercer it was!!!! We decided not to even venture to Kentucky. Macon just seemed like the right fit for our little family.

You might say that I was lucky to find employment so quickly in Macon. Paul tried to tell me when I got my advanced degree in behavioral disorders that I would only be offered jobs in that field. It turned out that there were lots of other openings in exceptional child education, but the administration in Macon determined that teaching in a specialized class for behaviorally challenged children was the job for me. They thought I would be a good fit. And I was.

As we went home and started to get things ready to move, I began to feel a bit of fear and trepidation. I had not been away from home before. When I was in college at Gardner Webb University, I was only about forty-five minutes from home. We had yard sales and sold items at the Flea Market and cashed in our retirement to finance this adventure. I guess you could say it was a bittersweet time but I kept having this feeling that the rug was being pulled out from under me.

Leaving Cherryville

The day prior to our move was special. We had all our boxes packed and labeled. We had taken our furniture apart as much as possible. We went to Gastonia to rent a U-Haul truck. Remember, we had very little funds so no fancy movers for us. We pulled the truck as close as possible to the front of our house to load. I really enjoyed using hand trucks to move a refrigerator. I've got it…have you got it…no…oh hell… Then we kept putting in boxes and packing that truck until—OMG, the truck was full and we were not done. We pulled our mattresses out into the yard and more boxes. We had to take off to Gastonia quickly to get a bigger truck before U-Haul closed. I was crying and cussing at the same time. Paul was just cussing. We made it and returned with the truck only to find that the neighborhood dogs had pissed on our mattress. This ranks in the top five worst days of my life.

Moving has always been a *real pain in the ass for me*. My marriage to my first husband, Tina Dawn's dad, was a whole messy three years. That is a whole book within itself. Once we determined it was time to untie the knot, my parents exercised some tough love and gave me two weeks to move out. Mom helped me find an affordable apartment near Gardner Webb College (now Gardner Webb University) where I was attempting to raise a child, work part time in Dad's law office, and graduate in three years. My parents did a lot to help me especially since I dashed their dreams by getting pregnant, quickly married, and quickly divorced. During this delightful move, a bunch of my Gardner Webb buddies helped me move from Gardner Webb back to my parents' home in Cherryville. No one told me to lash the doors closed on my lovely armoire. As I looked out the truck window, *I yelled, oh F..., yes you know what I said. I was watching all my cute clothes fly out of the back of the truck through the open doors on the armoire. Yes, I SO love to move.*

The next day, still tired and crazed, we took off for Macon. Paul and our dog, Opie Sugarlips, drove the U-Haul. Our friends the Goldbergs had their van. One of the Goldberg daughters, Margaret, rode with me, bless her heart. I had to drive by O'Dell's Grocery, (the place with the "Girlie Magazines") and go in and cry and had to go to both filling stations, Johnny Reynolds and Ralph Sellers, to cry not to mention having already cried at Hack Georges where Mom and Dad always bought gas. During my high school years, he always had the scoop on my goings on and would tattle tell on me to Dad. I, at least got to have some carnal pleasure with his nephew, while at Gardner Webb. Oh, well, at least with all the crying and snotting, I had the bon voyage gift from the

Goldbergs to make me feel better. They gave me a golden dove charm to signify that I would *"fly back to them." This touched my heart.* It seemed like a forever drive.

When we got there, you will think I am prone to exaggeration, but it was over 100 degrees. Summer is not the best time to move to Macon. To top it off we were on the third floor of this apartment complex. The Goldbergs and Bells (Annie Mae and Paul) began the hellish task of navigating those stairs with furniture and boxes. After struggling a little, Mary and the girls had a great idea. The women folk should venture out to find cold beverages and ice for The Group. This is still a sore spot with Paul. He says we were gone for hours while he, Leonard, and the Goldbergs son, Neal moved all the rest of the stuff. Well, we girls did not know our way around Macon. We did not happen to notice the little convenience store on the corner. I guess we did drive around a bit. When we returned, we found out that I had inadvertently put a bag of garbage on the truck. Neal had carried it up three flights of stairs. Somehow our iron skillets got lost in the move. How the Hell does one lose something as heavy as skillets?

It is at times like this when you know who your true friends are. The Goldbergs traveled all that way and helped us move. That was no easy task but there they were. No wonder that they have been lifelong friends. I still look at my golden dove charm and marvel at the depth of that friendship.

Tenants on the Uprising

———•———

Paul and I settled into our apartment and were curious about meeting all our new neighbors and adjusting to life in Macon. There was a little stir that we called, "tenants on the uprising." Our landlord bought the apartments as a senior's complex. They began to let non-seniors infiltrate, but we heard we were "the last straw" we had the nerve to bring a child into the complex! Truth is though that rumor was short lived. Tina Dawn was precious, and we figured we would get in great shape going up and down those stairs. We met the nice lady neighbor across the hall. She wasn't there a lot. We found out that she was there as someone's mistress for the occasional lover's quickie. Can't really tell you that she was someone notable because her presence there was a secret known to very few.

We met our downstairs neighbors, a couple who were both interesting and retired. She was a former librarian, and he had an eighth-grade education and a vast knowledge from all the places he traveled during WWII. He and Paul always had to be teammates during Trivial

Pursuit because they could rack up all the questions on geography. The couple met at Alcoholics Anonymous and fell in love.

The other pair of downstairs neighbors were a retired brother and sister. She could sew like mad and ended up making Tina Dawn lots of Barbie clothes. The brother was quite feeble and required us to run downstairs frequently to pick him up when he fell. When they had to give it up and move into a nursing home, we got sisters; one of which was in Mercer Law School with Paul.

Out in the garage upstairs were Keith and his wife. Keith was a "hoot." He always had a caper going on. He liked to repel the senior citizens high rise next door. He and Tina Dawn spent time on his roof spying on the neighbors with binoculars. One night he set off primer cord with black powder and blew a gigantic hole in the driveway. Tina Dawn was so excited the next day that Keith had made her a swimming pool. Keith also took flight lessons. That is a whole series of other stories.

On one side of the basement apartments was the "Dope Whore." This is sad and un-neighborly, but I truly do not remember her real name. As you may have guessed, she did a large number of drugs. One night she went out to her car and opened the car door and just stood there, like for hours. I guess she forgot what to do next. Keith and Paul were calling each other to look out. It was amazing to see.

I have saved my favorite neighbor for last. That was Miss Myrtle. Don't know why we always said "Miss." Her deceased husband was Saul, who she adored and called a "man's man." She had been a bookkeeper, and she was quite brilliant. She kept up with all the news and loved to have long conversations with Paul to get his point of view on world affairs. She lived during the days of speakeasies, where one would go and buy illegal liquor during Prohibition. There was a window that a customer would approach to "speak easy," perhaps a code word to gain admittance. Miss Myrtle had beautiful costume jewelry from that age. She had great stories from the past. She liked to have a bit of medicinal Early Times. Early Times is a brand of liquor and of course, she just had a nip now and then to ease joint pain and help her sleep. She would send me to buy it for her since she was a shut-in who had difficulty getting around. She, of course, had me make sure that it was in a brown paper bag so the neighbors could not see it. They might mistake its medicinal value for something else. She also loved Nu Way hotdogs and Long John Silver's fish and chips. She would have me pick her up food from time to time. Once Tina Dawn moved in and started school down the street, she really enjoyed Tina Dawn coming in after school. It was great for us since little eight-year-old Tina Dawn was a "latch key" kid and neither of us were home when she got home from school.

Paul's parents, Yoke and Bull, who were back home in North Carolina, volunteered to bring Tina Dawn to Macon after we got ourselves established in the apartment and knew our way around a bit. Tina Dawn stayed in Cherryville for most of the summer with her dad, my first husband. That was a brave undertaking for them since Tina Dawn was "voluntold" about the move to Macon. She, of course, did not have a say in the matter. Paul wanted this opportunity, and I wanted it for him. It was hard for her to leave home and her dad behind. She was used to seeing him every other weekend. Moving to a once a month or so visit was huge for her.

Having Tina Dawn arrive tearfully was difficult, but we did get to spend a little weekend time showing off our limited knowledge of Macon to Paul's parents. Oh wow, I knew the unemployment office, since I had no summer work and applied for food stamps. I had to call every week to talk to them about the jobs I had. What jobs? Well, Paul and I did get to know the Macon Mall too. We were there on our first visit. Paul was enjoying the fact that I knew no one in Macon and had to pretty much stay home and behave. We just arrived at the mall and got on the escalator. I looked over and screamed out at the brother-in-law of my modeling agent from home. He had a cute, model girlfriend. We began to talk, and she clued me in on how to get modeling jobs in Macon right there at the mall. I thought this was just grand. Paul could not believe that in the state of Georgia I just had to run into someone I knew.

I am going to segway a little here from Macon life. Modeling, yes, the story is that I have this huge southern accent. My parents wanted it to go away so that I could be more cultured as a southern lady. When I turned 16, they tried to enroll me in *Charm School*. My good karma sure kicked in because believe it or not, *Charm School* was full and Mom signed me up for modeling classes. This was way better. Our instructor was awesome, and we had fun learning how to walk and pose. She taught us health and beauty secrets and helpful interview tips. That began a long enduring relationship with the instructor.

After our graduation ceremony, she gave us various modeling jobs and fashion shows. Once when modeling various fashions at sites across Charlotte, I ended up modeling a tractor. Not something you get to do every day. While at Gardner Webb, I made my only magazine cover, The Biblical Recorder. Aren't you impressed? No Sports Illustrated Swimsuit edition for me. We did still modeling in store windows and I worked in the Charlotte and Atlanta fashion marts modeling clothes for buyers. That was the first time that I had a boss that drank liquor right there on site. I thought she drank a lot of water but then found out later that it was vodka. The modeling business has a lot of strange twists and turns. It is not all glamor. I was fortunate when I went to model at the Atlanta market that I was able to work for the same company I worked for in Charlotte. My roommate was not as fortunate. She worked for one gent a total of 30 minutes before he went into the dressing room and tried to grope her.

I went to New York to try to make the big time. When I went to the modeling agency, the lady interviewing me asked me if I was sitting down. *That was a reference to the fact that I was short.* Then she proceeded to tell me that my only modeling talent could be *selling fried chicken in the deep south.* Yes, I was super humiliated, but I tucked tail and went back home to continue furthering my education but let's face it, getting that extra work later on in Macon really did pay off. We were able to take Tina Dawn out to eat a little. She enjoyed that but those times were few and far between on our budget. Poor Tina Dawn, no dad, no friends, and sometimes less than no money!

School Daze

Tina Dawn began her third-grade school year walking distance from our apartment at an older school building on Vineville Avenue. She was a minority in her school and was picked on from the very first day. There was only one other white girl in the class. It was just a cultural experience to adjust to. She was also "a grain of salt in a pepper shaker." When she would leave to walk home, students would follow her and taunt her. She had her necklace pulled off her neck and the beads flew. She was a tough little critter and would continue to Miss Myrtle's apartment. Miss Myrtle would greet her, give her a snack, and try to make things better. Tina Dawn had her key to our apartment around her neck on a string (latchkey kid) and could let herself in and do her homework until Paul and I managed to arrive. Even though things were tough, Tina Dawn tried not to complain too much. She did have one friend in her class and that helped some. This child also had parents who were the hippy type. They had a landscape business and also grew some great weed, I am told. We were so glad that those two girls bonded and had some fun playing together.

One day Tina Dawn had enough of being bullied. I am not sure to this day what the boy did, but his pants ended up in a tree between the school and the apartment. Our neighbor, Lois, one of the sisters witnessed this event and was amazed at Tina Dawn's prowess and at how fast the boy with no pants ran away.

I arrived at my inner-city school in Macon. I still did not know the gravity of the situation and how this would be a valuable cultural experience for me similar to what Tina Dawn was experiencing in our neighborhood school. When I moved into my classroom, I met my teacher assistant, Betty Mae. That's right, you had Annie Mae and Betty Mae both in the same room. The classroom did have a "Time Out" booth with a two-way window. That was something I had always wanted to be able to subdue violent students. She was not very excited about it. The last teacher, she said, was given a chance to get her pocketbook and go to the house (meaning she was fired) after she was witnessed "doing the nasty" with a parent in that very Time Out Room. Oh well, Hell, here we go. Just what is it about schools that create lust? I had just completed five years teaching in North Carolina and oh my. I just had to tell Betty Mae that I heard news of a principal and a teacher having a *little office delight* one day when another teacher knocked at the door. While that teacher was talking to the principal, he thanked the other teacher and handed her a manila envelope. Little did Teacher 2 know that the envelope contained *the panties* of Teacher 1!!!! After I disinfected the "Time Out Room," I decorated and explained to Betty Mae about conducting class meetings. Some educators call this the Morning Meeting. That is a meeting you have with your students first thing in the morning to teach a social skill, review rules and procedures and set the tone for the day. I also explained that I operated my classroom with a points and rewards system. I expected both of us to do reading and math groups with my guidance of course. She was like, "hum." Then I noticed she was wearing a rosary and counting the beads!

I was in culture shock. The PE teacher and I were the only whites in the school, and he wasn't there every day. I would walk into the Teacher's Lounge, and everyone would stop talking. I was just a grain of salt in a pepper shaker and that was hard for me. I was used to being popular and having tons of stories to tell and people to tell them to. I was not used to being singled out and not given a chance just because of the color of my skin.

Growing up in Cherryville, I was a child in the fifties and had experienced racial prejudice. The sign in front of the laundromat said, "whites only" and one of the local restaurants was owned by clansmen and would put salt into the coffee if blacks tried to order there. I had a student's IEP (individual education plan for a student with a disability) signed by the parent as The *Esteemed Clansman*. When our family went to Myrtle Beach Buffy, our black maid, was always with us. There were restrooms and restaurants that she was not allowed to go into. All these things made me very sad as a child. At least, in elementary school when we integrated, things were smooth. The only ruckus caused was by some folks from a nearby town trying to stir up racial strife. Now, here I was in Macon, Georgia in the 80's seeing that old struggle still continues and getting to feel what it really feels like to be in the minority. Really made me think and continue to think. As I am editing this fictional adult memoir, it is Martin Luther King Day and we still have a lengthy path to equality.

Our very first day of school, I got to meet my students, Maney, Dick, Able, Mark, Norm and Mulan and Morton. Yes, they were all boys but that was not unusual in a class for behaviorally challenged students. We had our first Class Meeting and while I was putting the points on the board, Maney leaped to the floor and bit me on the Achilles tendon. He is a lucky boy to still have his teeth. Yes, when I got home that day I cried a river.

The next day went a little better. The boys could see that I was giving them points for their work and participation and was trying to make learning fun. That day, out on the playground, Dick (a very big elementary student) refused to come off the playground and was writhing around in the dust. My school was in the middle of a very dusty playground with no shade. I tried my best to get Dick inside. Ms. Betty Mae just took the other boys and went on in. Big Dick and I finally made it inside. We were both sweaty and dusty and then he began to hit me. Betty and I put him in Time Out. He was like a raging bull and broke the lock on the door.

Would I ever make it to Friday? My reward, remember we had less than no money, was going to be to walk to the convenience store down the block and buy a "champipple." That is what I called my little tiny bottle of Malt Duck, a cheap malt beverage.

Yes, I went home again on Tuesday and cried myself to sleep. This was very hard on Paul. Tina Dawn and I tried to keep our crying away from Paul. We were afraid he would drop out or flunk out. It was going to be a VERY long year.

In the midst of mine and Tina Dawn's daily angst over work and school, we had a reprieve in sight. At least Labor Day was coming!!!! My parents loved to square dance. They went to classes a couple of times per week and were part of a Square Dance Club. This year the club was going to dance in Gatlinburg and we were invited. We three, Paul, Tina Dawn and I piled up in our little Datsun B210 and took off to the mountains of Tennessee. When we arrived, we had a bit of car trouble. So glad that Paul is so good at fixing things. He was out in the hot sun repairing that car. He had to change the thermostat. He went to Napa and got the part. There were 4 screws in the thermostat. He got three back in and all went to Hell. He dropped the fourth screw. Much later, he was still cursing in the parking lot of the hotel while we went out to eat. Yes, a typical repair job until the last screw.

At least we were staying in a nice motel with a pool walking distance to town. We got to eat out every meal.

Tina Dawn had a ball and was spending her Pa Pa's money right and left. That is nothing unusual. When she first learned to talk, he was driving her through Cherryville and she spied Odell's store and said, "Pa Pa, see that sign. It says, *we sell candy here!* "Of course, she couldn't read but Dad whipped his Cadillac in and bought his precious little favorite granddaughter some candy. That is exactly how he handled shopping in Gatlinburg. She loved to buy these little "grab bags" for $5.00. She did not know what would be inside. Yes, a rip-off but she loved it, and Dad indulged her. I cannot disparage Tina Dawn. I was spending Mom's money. She knew I was crying every day after work, so she bought me a new outfit with jewelry to match. That weekend sure lifted our spirits for a few days.

We trudged our way back into the various schools (law school, Hell School, and Hell School) and tried to keep our chins up as we counted off the days till the next holiday.

Can You Mix Without a Mixer?

———•·———

Paul and I were invited to a "mixer" at Mercer School of Law (a.k.a. Walter F. George School of Law). The school was founded in 1873 and is one of the oldest law schools in the country. The building is one of the most recognizable sites in Macon, as it is a three-story replica of Independence Hall in Philadelphia and is located on top of Coleman Hill overlooking downtown Macon. At the time it served about four hundred students, and the purpose of the mixer was to give the new incoming class of law students and their spouses or significant others a chance to meet and get to know each other prior to the start of classes.

It is amazing that Paul told me about the mixer, since he does not enjoy large group social events. Why did they use the term "mixer"? That does sound really *Old South*, even to me. We knew that would mean we could meet others that he would be in class with. We parked and followed the signs. The view from Coleman Hill was spectacular. Just standing there, even in the August heat, the sight over the hill was captivating and I felt good to be a part of this new city.

The first couple that introduced themselves to us were William and his girlfriend, Anne. They were high school sweethearts. They both went to private school in Macon. William was an athlete and played football well enough to get to play at the University of Georgia following graduation. His mother died of cancer and his dad, who was a well-healed banker in Macon, remarried a much younger beautiful trophy wife with two children. Anne was also athletic and was a high school sharpshooter in ROTC. Her parents divorced and her mother remarried. They were both young and attractive and their parental issues even made them closer. Their wedding was right after law school graduation. I learned of a southern tradition at their wedding. Did you know that it is an honor to be chosen to serve the cake at a wedding? I always thought it was work, and messy work at that. Well, I got that honor.

William and Anne were standing with another couple who introduced themselves as Tim and Vergie. William called him Timmy. It was obvious that they already knew each other. They were high school friends, and both went to college at the University of Georgia.

It turns out that Tim and Vergie met at Freshman Orientation for honor students at the University of Georgia. Vergie was in a bit of a dilemma because she had a former boyfriend who was also at Georgia. They had broken up during their senior year of high school. He tried to rekindle the flame by asking Vergie to attend his brother's wedding as his date. Vergie had to make a tough decision. I don't know about you but I so remember how brightly those high school flames burn. You really think that its true is love. It is a trying time. Do you say yes to one and leave the other behind? That line is even in a golden oldie song. Vergie had to focus hard on trying to meet and greet the many cute eligible guys at Georgia and not look back. Getting back to orientation, Vergie attended before actually making up her mind. She went downstairs from her dorm room and struck up a conversation with Tim from Macon, Georgia. Needless to say, she decided against dating her former boyfriend again. Much later, as it turned out, the former boyfriend leaped out of the closet and was gay. Maybe no other woman was as beautiful or alluring as Vergie. Vergie did say that she did not think it was the loss of her affection that rendered him gay. We all are so glad that Vergie met Tim and never looked back. I knew as soon as I met them that they belonged together.

Paul, Tim, and William all had classes together, so guy banter ensued. The guys kept picking on each other and extended their targets to other students who joined the exchange.

We met guys named Mel, Natty, and Hugh but everybody was calling Hugh by his last name, Vinelli. We met Georgia and her husband, Ephraim. Georgia was older. She must have been in the "interesting character" group that got in like Paul. When Paul went on his interview, the interviewer said that most law students get admission due to good grades or a great score on the LSAT, law entrance exam or they, like Paul were considered for admission because they were "interesting characters," we met other law students and their significant others, one thing became obvious to me. Most everyone was young and fresh out of college. We were not ancient but had been out of college awhile and we had a child. Everyone was nice enough though. I don't usually have anxiety at these things but I did feel a little like a fish out of water. I was a small-town girl and did not feel as intelligent or worldly as this group. The crowd thickened and the guys and girls separated.

I found out that we womenfolk, except those who were the female law students, would have get- togethers with the "law wives." That sounded like it could be fun, and as time went by it was. Once we all went to a Pampered Chef party together. We were all so poor that the hostess probably did not come out with much in the way of perks. Believe it or not I bought a clay baking stone and still love it. Another gathering was at a lingerie party. That should have been pretty good since William and Anne were engaged. The problem yet again, was the absence of funds. Anne and I both tried on a black gown with lace. The fit was "to die for" and both of us looked classy and slutty at the same time. That is a hard combo to achieve. We still talk about that gown that neither of us could afford. Finally, we had a meeting that was a recipe swap. This was Vergie's idea and was a winner. Now, we could all get into this. Most of the recipes only contained a few ingredients and none were very expensive. I remember getting a recipe for fettuccine Alfredo. It had parmesan cheese that you made and ate over fettuccine noodles. It was good and affordable, and I think of Vergie each time I prepare that dish.

In the meantime, the guys were settling into their classes. Tina Dawn and I tried to keep a low profile. We did not want anything to get in the way of Paul's success in his classes. Paul came home and related over dinner that the first day one of the professors had said, "Look on each side of you, one of you will not graduate." That was pressure. I woke up in the middle of that night and thought that if I slipped and fell there would be no source of income. I woke up first thing the next day and purchased disability insurance.

Paul said the students were given law cases to read and "debrief" meaning that were able to give the facts of the case and the applicable case law. The students were intimidated and did not want to be called on. Paul was known to put a note on a professor's desk to inform them that it was William's birthday. Professors usually called on students on their birthdays. Paul enjoyed giving William these un-birthday "gifts," as William would get very flustered when called upon. Once, according to Paul, when William was asked in which state the case was tried, William responded, "Omaha." The professor re-asked the question, "William, in which state was this case tried?" and William fervently responded, "The **state** of Omaha." He was not clued in to the state of Nebraska. The professor was not amused and said that William was obviously in a "state of confusion", while Paul quietly snickered in his seat.

Paul drew a regular cartoon with William featured as Mr. Music and Tim featured as Mr. Law Review. William knew lots about music and he was proud that the Allman Brothers were from Macon, his hometown. He took Paul out to Rose Hill cemetery to show him the grave of Dwayne Allman and expostulated on everything he knew about the Allman Brothers Band. Paul kept telling William he had never heard of Dwayne Allman. The Allman what? What did they play? Of course, after William named all the songs and was just aghast, Paul relented that he in fact did know who the Allman Brothers were and that he was a fan. Paul could play multiple songs of theirs on the guitar.

Tim was focused and a gunner who just had to make Law Review, a special honor awarded to the law students who showed proficiency in briefing cases. Tim was quite smart and studied hard. We were proud of him and of Paul, who were part of Moot Court which was also an honor. The guys were proud of their accomplishments but still had to make fun of each other constantly and with vigor.

The girls enjoyed time together also. We would put together meals from whatever we had in the refrigerator,

"You have corn? We have some beans…" "I have milk, do you have cereal?" We needed each other to navigate our law school years. Would we have eventually mixed without the mixer? Hmmm. I'm glad we mixed and that there would be mischief in Macon to be had with our newly found friends.

The Scout Promise

On my honor, I will try... Scouting was such a part of my childhood. My dad and brother were Eagle Scouts and Paul had a history of scouting also. My brother was a lifeguard at a scout camp in Tryon, North Carolina. I just idolized him and his friends. There was a family night and we got to visit. Tryon, back before better highways, had a curvy mountain road. It did not make Mom and Dad happy that I *puked my guts out* in the car on the way. When we arrived, I was a hot and smelly mess with vomit on my white tee shirt. My brother was eight years older, but I still fell in love with his friends. It was so embarrassing that Pukey Annie Mae wanted to flirt with the Fire Dancer. He was doing a Native American dance as part of their program that night. I did not know, at that time, that my brother never wanted his friends to strike up a relationship with me. He told his friends that I had *no little toes*. I could not understand why they would ask to see my feet. It was just natural that I would also be a scout and expect Tina Dawn to follow the family tradition and have "scouting" in her blood.

Paul was also a scout and just missed also being an Eagle. We both had our scout sashes proudly showing off our badges.

Since Paul and I both grew up in scouting, it was only natural that we would get Tina Dawn involved in scouting. In our former life in North Carolina, Tina Dawn was a brownie. She was in a troop that met after school. She participated in all the activities, and we have a couple of cute pictures in her album. Ann was Tina Dawn's friend who lived down the street in Macon. I found out her mother had a scout troop. Here we go!!! I joined her up and became Assistant Scout Leader. I felt that I had the background to be a good assistant leader, but that history is a little sketchy.

One summer, prior to getting my driver's license, I was a counselor at Girl Scout Day Camp. One of the local scout leaders (not my troop leader) picked me up each morning. She had the longest, curviest fingernails I had ever seen. I was not familiar at that time with manicures. She also had a china cup of coffee with her each morning and her hand shook most of the coffee out. She had a large house and was an animal lover. She even had a pony that lived inside. These attributes made me feel that she was to the "beat of a different drummer" and embezzlement became part of her future. Now, my local scout leader had 3 daughters and a host of foster children. We did many projects at her house, and I had a great time and earned many badges. One time we painted a jeep for a project.

As one of my projects, I wanted to plant a little birch tree from my grandmother's farm in our back yard. We got the little tree and brought it to the house. Now, as part of this story, you have to know about Buffy. She was my "other mother." Now, she was a short but hefty black lady who was feisty, filled with fire and full of energy. Back then, in the south, she was known as our maid. Today, she would be the nanny. She cooked for us, looked after us every day while the parents were at work, and taught us many things about life. She was my heart and soul. On this particular day, as I was getting a big shovel out of the basement, she was calling her grandson. He was about 12 years old like me and we were friends. She told him to come to my house to dig a hole and plant my little tree. My brother walked out and said that his *little white sister* was going to dig that hole and plant that tree while we all watched. It was quite a spectacle, but I dug that hole and planted that damn tree. It was there in our yard and my project was complete and I did not die in the process. My tree was a big deal for our family. We stood in front of MY tree and took our family pictures every year.

Our scout troop loved to work on badges in the woods and would go to a place called the Big Ditch. We had many an excursion there. We practiced building fires, putting on bandages and carrying each other out of the woods. I did get in big trouble once at the Big Ditch. One of the girl's little sisters followed us into the woods. We ran around and did our thing and just left her there in the woods. When we got home and she didn't, there was HELL to pay. Thank God she was found and was OK. Not a great thing for a scout to do.

You cannot be Girl Scouts without cookies. I could remember all our neighbors on Elm Street buying lots of cookies when I was a Girl Scout in Cherryville. Tina Dawn did have our sweet neighbors in our Macon senior citizen home, but they were mostly diabetic, and she wanted to sell LOTs of cookies. Down the street from our Vineville neighborhood was a cute little neighborhood named Ingleside Village. It had our laundromat, a bakery, our church, and a beauty shop. Tina Dawn eagerly took off down to the village. She was thrilled because she sold LOTs of cookies. There was a problem though, she had the names of people and their money but *no* addresses. Once we picked up her cases of cookies, we just had to leave a pile of them at the beauty shop and just hope and pray that the owners became matched up with their cookies.

One of the great things about scouts is going to camp. Our little Macon troop was very much excited to go to overnight camp. Now, when I went to camp, we had to dig latrines to use as a potty and we slept outside cooking our food over a fire. Our Macon troop was staying in a cabin. I could not believe it. Not roughing it at all. My favorite laugh of the weekend was when Ann's mom got me up one morning and said that we needed to go outside to get ready for the jungle breakfast. I thought, here we go, we are going to cook outside. Oh no, we were hiding boxes of cereal and milk for them to find. That was a jungle breakfast.

Our troop was invited to participate in a large event that was about introducing the girls to safe sex. What???? Boy, scouting was different, but OK. Ann's mom drove the troop over to the event and I was to pick them up at the end. They were hilarious. The four of them decided to sit in the back seat. No one sat up in the front seat with me. All the way back, they talked about sex and would take their fingers and put them in the air for the "hard on" and take them down for the "not ready." I was watching them in the rear-view mirror. Boy, scouting has really changed.

Now, back during my childhood in Cherryville, my childhood friend Mildred got the idea that since we were such good Methodists that we should go to church camp at Camp Tekoa. Our parents thought that was a stellar idea so off we went. It was so different from Girl Scout camp. Cabins with bathhouses, a pool, a lake, and boys. Yes, I said it. Boys. Holy Cow, during vespers I said a lot of prayers of thanks for the boys. Our counselor was so handsome, I had a big crush on him too. I was so proud that I swam the length of the pier and passed the swim test. I got to go out in the deep part of the lake where the diving platform was and yes, you guessed it. The boys congregated there. We even had a campout at the end of the week—*yes, the boys were there all night.* From that moment on, I was done with scout camp. Only church camp for me. No more Girl Scout cookies. Church camp fundraisers, here I come. Thank you, Mildred.

Fire, Theft, Drowning, and Feet, Don't Fail Me Now

———◆———

Betty Mae, my teacher assistant, and I were having an up and down time with our boys. Our students that were on the uphill climb in terms of good days and points were awarded each month with a variety of activities. At the end of each week the boys got to choose prizes from our School Store. The teachers had to buy the prizes. Paul and Tina Dawn about died ten thousand deaths at the expenditure for their prizes, but hell, it was necessary to keep my school life afloat. You may call it bribery, but that is payment for wrongdoing. This was payment for right-doing. Good grief, Betty Mae and Annie Mae, neither one would be there without pay!!!!

Betty Mae and I always tried to at least be on a positive note first thing in the morning, but some days our day was wrecked by 8:30. One day, the office called and said, "Bell, get to the auditorium." I went and there was the smoldering auditorium curtain with the custodian trying to put out the fire and the principal trying to run down

Morton. Yes, I did say "run." Morton had brought in a cigarette lighter and set the curtain on fire prior to coming to class.

There was poor Principal Hutley, not a young man, trying to run down the wiry, lightning fast, Morton with students yelling, "Go, Morton, go." I broke into a run too so we could try to hem him in. Well, Bless Pat, poor Principal Hutley fell and was writhing on the ground. Hum.... Do I keep running or drop back to help Hutley?

There, thankfully, was the PE teacher saying, "I got Hutley, you get Morton." Well, thank you NOT but I did keep running. In those days I was really fast. That is why I was the leadoff batter in softball. Before you knew it, Morton and I were rolling around on the auditorium floor just outside the office building. Thankfully, teachers came in and out of the office and came to render assistance. Our social worker, Mr. Lindsay, was there too and helped me talk to Morton. Mr. Lindsay knew all about Morton and his whole family due to many home visits. Principal Hutley was taken to the doctor. He had hurt his leg. Man, oh man, I was just glad it was not a heart attack!!!! Mr. Lindsay took Morton home for a day of out of school suspension and so that he could regale the family with how lucky Morton was not to be arrested for starting a fire in the auditorium and incapacitating our principal.

Yet again early one morning, Betty Mae whispered to me that I might want to look in Morton' book bag.

Really? Seriously? *Oh, yes.* I was looking at each student's morning work and having individual conferences with them. Finally, I sauntered over to Morton. Let's look at your work this morning. Oh, my heart began to beat. I could see a pile of envelopes inside his desk. "Oh, what have we here?" I took them out. Morton had managed to walk through the office this morning and he had stolen ALL the payroll checks. We took them to the office. Principal Hutley just shook his head. I mean, sometimes there are just no words.

Of course, I loved my class. Yes, they were rogues but all cute and loveable. I think that Principal Hutley loved them too deep down inside and I know that Betty Mae did. Another one of my students was Maney. Maney's family was Muslim. They had advised that they did not want him celebrating any holidays. That is so hard with the little ones. We did a lot of holiday things and Betty Mae and I just let Maney decide if he wanted to be involved or not, whatever he chose but we kept a low profile and would try to be a little generic. Our whole school was invited to a Thanksgiving assembly. Some classes sang and Principal Hutley did a presentation. He had a giant paper turkey up front with feathers that had to be added on as made his speech. Yes, you guessed it. He selected Maney to be his assistant and put the feathers on the turkey as he talked. Usually, Betty Mae and I would beam if our students got any schoolwide glory, but we were both horrified and seeing our lives pass right by before our eyes. Maney strutted up front like the cock of the walk and he did a super job with the turkey. Luckily, his family was OK with all that. I do think they trusted us to do right by Maney. They were so pleased with me that they invited me to visit their masque and to model in their fashion show fundraiser. Of course, I was pleased as punch and said yes.

Crazy Annie Mae and Betty Mae decided to take our students to a camp operated by the district. The students were so excited, and we sent home lists of what they needed to bring to camp. The big day came and Principal Hutley came in and prayed over us. We loaded the bus. We pulled out of the school parking lot and proceeded toward the road and headed in the direction of the camp. The students began to yell, "Mrs. Bell, isn't that Morton running behind the bus?" I jumped up and looked out of the window. "Holy Hell, yes that is Morton." Bless his little sticky-fingered, thieving, fire-starting heart, he was running as fast as he could behind the bus. I am sure he was thinking, *feet, don't fail me now.* "Stop the fucking bus!!!" I snatched him up on the bus and hugged him so tight. To this day, no matter who I am with I count people to make sure that all are present.

We arrived at camp. The students' favorite thing was the food. The cafeteria let them eat all they could. They had all sorts of activities for them to do. We had stories, arts and crafts and of course water sports like canoeing. Dick had the knack of getting on everyone's nerves. One day Dick kept picking on Morton. Morton finally jumped off the bench and began to pummel Dick. I did intervene but *very s-l-o-w-l-y.* Sometimes natural consequences were the best. Dick was so pesky that quite frequently I had to go to an area and eat with only Dick.

One afternoon the whole group was so excited. We were going to have a canoe race across the lake. Guess who did not have a partner? You guessed it. Dick was my partner. As a teacher, sometimes you just do what you have to do. Off we went. Hey, this was great. Yes, he was big, and our canoe was quickly in the lead. We were moving way away from the others headed toward the finish line. Dick was paddling like a champion, but he leaned over just a little too far and *over we went. Canoe upside down in the water.* Dick was sputtering and floundering. The camp lifeguards were quick to the rescue and Dick, and I went over to the bank. Our canoe was brought in. Dick and I were soaked. Dick had used up all his camp clothes and had to put on my turquoise warm up suit. The legs came to his knees and the sleeves to his elbows. He was a sight to behold. *He looked like a giant Easter jelly bean.* WE WERE THE ONLY BOATING ACCIDENT THE CAMP HAD EVER HAD.

Proms and Proposals

———•———

Is it proms or proposals? Maybe it should be things little girls dream of all their lives. I just don't know. I think love and romance are so fascinating. You heard early on the story of Vergie and Tim. They met at Freshman Orientation in college and fell deeply in love and never looked back. They have an enduring relationship. Mine and Paul's proposal of marriage was a lot like William and Anne's. Now, you remember William, Paul's law school buddy? Let's just say he's not a planner. Anyway, William and Anne were on the way to a dinner party at Tim and Vergie's. William had decided that this was the perfect moment to say those magic words. You know those words that every little girl dreams about.

According to Anne, the time had come, and William said, "Anne, open the glove compartment. Do you want to have a go at it?" I think you'll agree that no more romantic words have ever been spoken. Not.

Anne opened the glove compartment and spotted the box with the engagement ring in it. She put it on and said, "Yes, I would like to have a go at it." She sashayed into Vergie's and Tim's sporting her engagement ring which was a family heirloom. The women in the room shrieked, looked at it longingly and carried on like they had just seen their favorite Hollywood actor. Vergie had made a wonderful meal of fettuccine. It was always one of my favorites. I was so excited that she was serving it, and you need to try it.

Fettuccine Alfredo
1 lb. fettuccine noodles, 1 stick butter, 1 C heavy cream, salt and pepper to taste, 2 C grated parmesan.

Cook pasta according to directions, Warm butter and cream and season with salt and pepper.

Put half grated parmesan in a bowl and pour warm butter and cream over it.

Drain pasta and pour into bowl and toss a few times and then sprinkle with remaining cheese.

We all were amused about William's romantic proposal and then I told them about Paul's proposal.

We started dating in October, and it was January, so we had been dating for about three months. We were in the parking lot of the mall in Gastonia, North Carolina, when he asked if I would marry him. Well, this was not exactly the proposal I had dreamed of as a little girl, but of course, I said yes. The ring came along later.

Now, back to William and Anne's wedding. Paul still contends to this day that he did not attend William and Anne's wedding. We know and have proof that he was there. He was in their wedding pictures. You know how there are things little girls dream of weddings and proposals are not at the top of a guy's fun things to do list. I don't know how he can't remember. It was your typical southern wedding with mints, punch, and peanuts. That is all you expected back in the day. Now this part of the story *is not* your typical southern wedding. Anne's neighbor made the wedding cake. She froze four layers of the five-layer cake. The top layer was the one you freeze to eat on your first anniversary. The day before the wedding, she put the frozen layers on the table to thaw. The custodian suggested that she put them under the table so they would not be disturbed. The day of the wedding, she got the top layer ready and the columns to support it. She lovingly got the now thawed layers from under the table and OH MY GOD, ants swarmed up her arms. What to do? Anne's mother discreetly got Anne's hair dryer and used a toothpick to remove all the ants from their sugary repose. The cake was salvaged, and according to Anne's mother, no guest was the wiser.

Now that you have heard about our lame non-romantic proposals, here is the real deal.

This is a romantic story, I think. This is a story about William's aunt. Elizabeth Runyan (Sissy) was Miss East Point and captain of her high school basketball team. She continued her basketball career after graduation and traveled to Alabama with her Allstar team. During a basketball trip to Alabama, she was destined to meet her one true love, Bill Runyan. The two fell for each other immediately, and she went to visit him in Oklahoma where he was stationed for flight training. While she was there, he received orders and was to ship out to put his bomber training into action with the Fifteenth Air Force flying bomber missions to foil German progress in WWII. Bill immediately proposed that they marry before he had to leave.

A local Baptist church learned about Bill and Sissy's engagement and within three weeks created a beautiful wedding for them, complete with a wedding dress, a full reception including a cake, and the congregation serving as witnesses. Her sister, Kathleen, was the only family member who was able to travel there by train because of the train restrictions in place at the time. Bill and Sissy were married for six weeks before he deployed. Sissy returned to Atlanta to wait out the war.

Bill piloted his B-17 through 15 missions from North Africa to Italy, Germany, and in notorious raids including the bombing of Ploiesti Oil Fields in Romania. After the invasion of Italy, Bill's squadron moved to an airfield in southern Italy. In the summer of 1944, he was a fill-in pilot on a raid against a ball-bearing plant in Milan. During the raid, their plane was hit by flack and suffered enough damage that their speed was reduced. They fell further and further back from the formation as they returned from the raid and were jumped on by three FE-109 Messerschmitt.

Bill's crew was able to shoot down one plane, but they sustained so much damage from attacks, the crew was forced to abandon their burning plane. From the accounts of the two survivors of the ultimate plane break up, the navigator put a parachute on an unconscious airman and went forward to inform the pilot they were the last two to leave the plane, and it was time for Bill to leave. Bill said I will keep the plane steady while you get free. As the airman worked to get the other guy out, the plane exploded, and Bill perished.

The village priest recovered Bill's body and buried it in the church cemetery knowing the Fascists, the Black Shirts, would soon be there to search the crash site for survivors. He contacted Sissy after the war ended and told Sissy they saw what happened to the plane from the ground and the plane was under control as it came down. Bill had missed the village and the church and crashed in a field. The priest returned Bill's ring, his watch, and his dog tags. He showed her the farm where the plane crashed. The farmers had used the wing of the plane as a roof for their pigsty and the tire as a feeding trough. Sissy had Bill's body moved and interred in the U.S. Cemetery in Rome. She wore Bill's watch for years and years.

Bill's nickname was Sleepy. He died in 1944. She never remarried.

To this day Sissy's family cherishes Bill's Purple Heart, his Bronze Star, his Distinguished Air Medal, his flight cap, his personal items locker, his flight wings, and the flag that covered his coffin when they moved it to the U.S. cemetery in Rome. A niece owns the strand of pearls Sissy wore at her wedding and another niece wears her wedding ring. A nephew owns a bracelet that is engraved "Sissy" on one side and "Sleepy" on the other.

Now, I am going to move this memoir to a tale of proms. My junior prom started with me on the decorating committee. Now for some reason I thought drinking before school was a good idea and would spur on my decorative artsy process. It was all fun and games until I ended up puking in my purse. You should have seen the look on Buffy's face when I got home with that hot mess. Let me tell you cleaning out that purse was no joke. All the girls looked forward to senior prom. Buying the dress was one of those things that little girls dream about. Purchasing the perfect dress was a big deal. Buying the dress is a big deal. Louise and I decided to go shopping together and we ended up purchasing matching halter dresses with big slits up the front. Our dresses were fabulous. They were cut down to the waist and slit almost to the waist. Louise's was navy blue and mine was green. My dad marveled at the low price until he saw the dress. Well, no wonder. They had about as much cloth as a napkin. I don't think Louise's dad ever saw her dress. My date was my first husband, Leon, go figure. He got in a real knock down drag out southern redneck brawl with his brother who was Louise's date. The fight started because Leon's brother was embarrassed because Leon did not rent a tux. Here my mom was trying to take my picture and all I could do was cry. Now you would think that the fight would be the end of the drama but, NO. Between the prom and the after party, Leon spent most of the night trying to find "weed, pot, Maryjane, whatever" that he hid and could not find. Do you wonder why that marriage did not last? And the cherry on top of this was that my parents were chaperones! I have to say it was truly a night to remember. Now, as if prom night was not bad enough, when I went to pick up my prom picture, there was not one for some reason. I did have my picture taken with a friend of mine and his mom has that picture as she often reminds me. And then there was college where I had Tina Dawn, and with a baby I attended no proms.

When Paul went to law school, this brings me to my jolt of ecstasy I experienced when I found out that Mercer had a Barrister's Ball, in essence, a lawyer's prom. A ball, a ball. Oh, Ladies and Gentlemen I had dreams of being Cinderella going to the ball. I ordered this beautiful gold dress that looked sort of like Marilyn Monroe. I was beyond excited until I was ready to go that night and realized that Paul did not buy me a corsage. What, no flowers? The Hell? I cried a river. The ball was me bawling my eyes out. This sounds so silly even as I am typing these words, but it was the truth. I sucked it up and we made it to the fancy dinner. Of course, I had not been out to a fancy formal dinner in forever. I was soaking up the grandeur when I noticed that the couple beside me was having a lewd and lascivious moment right there under the table. Oh, yes, it was a hand job. I was not the only one who noticed. Man, she was an amazing talent with that hand. Here again this takes "ball" to another level. Even though I didn't have a freaking corsage, we made it to the ball and danced the night away. I got over my old "sour puss" mood and well, fuck the flowers, it was a great time.

Proms and proposals may have certain connotations in one's point of view, in little girl's dreams or silly fairy tales, but it is really the relationship that matters in the long run. Vergie and Tim, William and Anne and Paul and I have all been happily married for over forty years.

The Haunting

---◆---

It was nice when the melting asphalt heat in Macon began to ebb into fall. The trees began to turn, and the air was crisp. A couple of my work friends liked to hang out at Central City Park. We would play pick-up football or softball. During one of our softball games, I decided it was time for me to cross something off my bucket list, chewing tobacco. Well, you know, a lot of ball player's chew. I figured there had to be something to it. Now, I did not want to be like those old southern women who dip and the brown stuff dribbles down their chin, but I did want to chew and be cool. Paul tried to dissuade me and said that chewing sunflower seeds sure seemed like a better option but oh hell no, I had to chew tobacco. I was out in right field with my little chaw in my jaw. Snuff dribbling down my chin might have been better than turning green and puking my guts out. I was just lucky that no one hit the ball my way. Oh yeah, marked that one off my list. Never to be done again. After the game, the girls decided to do something creative on this fall day. They decided that we should lie down on the ground forming curse words. We really did. We spelled out tit, twat, etc. Well, you get the general idea. I had cool friends in Cherryville, but Macon had a new level of creativity.

Soon the feel of Halloween began to fill the air and the costume shops. Halloween has always been one of my favorite holidays since Elm Street in Cherryville was so much fun. Most of the houses on the street participated and it was lots of fun. When Tina Dawn was little, we lived on Elm Street. She was not that fond of Trick or Treat because our street was literally a sea of children in costumes. She would walk out the door. Go to the house across the street and get a little candy. Then she would try to walk down Elm but just couldn't and would turn around and run home with us running behind her.

While in high school, tricks were as important as treats. The Group decided to trick the house of a girl from a rival high school. She had taken away one of our boyfriends and there should be Hell to pay. We dressed up like we were really going out trick or treating. My parents had escaped for the weekend and my grandmother and aunt were in charge of me. They thought it was fun that I was going out with the girls trick or treating. We went to a house first that had horses. I was selected to sneak through the fence and to shovel horse shit into a paper bag. Of course, I did and jumped back in the car, bag of shit and all. We went out to this girl's house. We left one of the girls in the car for a speedy getaway. The house was dark. We went onto the porch and placed our "treat" on the porch and as we were lighting it, all the lights came on and her Daddy came out with a shotgun and shot it. We literally flew off the porch in all directions, running and screaming. We ran to the ... oh, the car. Where is the car? Our getaway car had got up and went. We were running into a field as another shot rang out. We began to crawl. I remember praying that if God let me live, I would become a nun. At that time, I did not know that nuns were Catholic. As I crawled out of the field with one girl, we saw another girlfriend crawling out of a ditch. I could see my blue Chevelle in the distance, and I made a run for it and flagged it down. You have never seen girls getting into a car so fast. I realized that we smelled really bad, were quivering and my pantyhose were literally in shreds AND they and *my nether region were full of thorns.* When I got home, my grandmother and aunt were a bit perplexed. I just said that someone beat me up and took my candy away. As hellish as it was, it was still a great Trick or Treat night to remember.

Back at the school where I taught in North Carolina, we did a big, haunted house every year. That brings to mind my former principal. The day I met him for the first time, he was getting off a school bus, carrying a bucket and a mop and I thought he was either the bus driver or the custodian. At that time, he was the youngest principal in North Carolina. It just seems to me that most principals are male with a large staff that is mostly female. It is just like their own little harem. This principal would get out a wad of money to show me and say "is today the day" like he could pay me to do the nasty. Get out. Now, you might call that sexual harassment and oh yeah, by the way, it is but I just called it flirting. He was married but he was enamored of several on the staff and liked to tease. He also, though, was very strict, especially about signing in ON TIME.

One day, I was late for reasons beyond my control. Six-year-old Tina Dawn and I went out to get into the car to drive to work. Paul was still in bed. When I opened the car door, a Mexican fell out of the car door, halfway in and halfway out of the car, with his fly open.

I screamed and ran into the house. "Paul, help, there is a Mexican in our car with his fly open."

"And where is Tina Dawn?"

"Oh FUCK, I left her out there." I ran back frantically and she was fine. Tina Dawn said that he just wanted to use the phone. "How do you know that?"

"He picked up the CB radio and said 'Debda, debda, debda.'" That is what happens when you or your child neither know how to speak Spanish. Well, I guess he crawled in there to get warm. As a small-town girl, no, I did not have my car locked. Well, anyway, of course Tina Dawn and I were late for school and work. There stood the principal when I tried to sign in. He was mad.

"Well, I just couldn't help it. A Mexican fell out of my car with his fly open." Sure. Sure, he did. Imagine. He did not believe me... Anyway, back to haunted houses.

A group of NC teachers took the whole back wing of the building and made it into a haunted house. We charged money from the kids as a fundraiser. A more traditional Halloween Carnival was going on in the rest of the building, but our haunted house drew a huge crowd. We had all the favorites. The witches with the dry ice witch's brew in the cauldron and the mad scientist that had grapes for the kids to hold that were supposed to be eyeballs. But the greatest thing I have to say was Paul as the werewolf. He could do fantastic makeup. He made me up as the Hunchback of Notre Dame and I was in our little graveyard. He did his make up like the traditional Lon Chaney werewolf. He was an actor in old horror films. His little area was a bed with Grandma that the children went right up to and of course the werewolf came up behind them, and they were terrified. The next best thing was the table that Paul made. It was designed so that it looked like you were sawing the person in half with blood oozing out. Now, we were so excited that our haunted house was a big hit. Paul's sister Dawn was designated to take little Tina Dawn to the Carnival and of course, to our haunted house. They bought their tickets and stood in a long line. They could hear the children screaming. When it finally came time for them to enter, Tina Dawn turned tail and ran. Dawn never did get to see the full effect of our haunted house.

Of course, now in Macon, Paul and I talked incessantly about our former haunted house experience. Anne decided that we must do a haunted house at her school to raise money. Paul of course reprised his role as werewolf and me as hunchback. We joined right in with the staff at Anne's school. In this scenario, Paul was behind a partition which did fall at some point during the night. He was even scarier this time and the children were running and screaming. There was the Werewolf at one end of the hall and Frankenstein at the other end of the hall. After the partition fell and the students were between the two monsters, the kids were just running back and forth and screaming bloody murder. Paul had backed this large child into a corner with her feet just running in place. She finally gained traction and ran in a straight line knocking down the partition, the adults, and making her way to the exit with a catastrophe in her wake. The haunted house crew had to take a break to reset the scene. I guess, we were mighty damn lucky not to have been trampled to death.

Tina Dawn did enjoy getting Halloween candy since she was the only child in our building and teachers in my school and Anne's school wanted to treat her. She was very possessive of her candy. She knew we would ration it out.

The worst story ever was told by our friend Mark. He took his children's candy on Halloween night and gave them a couple of pieces to eat. He froze the candy so that the parents could parcel it out for them to eat over a period of time. The sweet children did not realize that after they went to bed every night, Mark was eating their candy. I don't think he really realized how much he was eating until it was all gone. He has not lived that down to this day. I guess he was a candy monster. That was a new one to me. Another friend did the Switch Witch. She would take her children's Halloween candy and make trades for coins while the kids were asleep. Now, what do you think of these "After Halloween" monsters torturing their children? I think it is just *wrong*.

Let's Be Thankful

Our Macon crew had a huge weekend planned. Now, thinking back on this, I have no idea how we afforded it, but William scored us tickets for a Beach Boys concert. YIPPEE. This was so exciting. We were to all go to Georgia's house (one of our law school buddies) and hang out and then head to Albany for the concert.

I mentioned earlier that Georgia was older than our crew, but she was tons of fun. One day she had an appointment somewhere in Macon. She was not from Macon and did not really know her way around. She made the mistake of asking William for directions. He was notorious for giving bad directions. Who in Hell's name asks William for directions? Poor Georgia must not have heard the tales of his misdirection. He told her to turn at a certain landmark. Georgia rode around for a long while and almost missed her appointment. The landmark had gone out of business a long while ago.... Georgia was a good sport though and let him live. Back in the day, Izod with the alligator was the designer brand to have. Everybody wore those damn alligators. It was an alligator embroidered on a polo shirt. Even the destitute law students managed to have a polo or two. Paul was never a designer kind of guy. He makes fun of anyone who was brainless enough to spend that kind of money on a freaking polo shirt with a stupid little alligator on it. That clever Georgia surprised Paul with a lavender polo shirt. He was crazed until he noticed that the alligator was a dead roach with its little roach feet in the air. Georgia had embroidered the roach!!!!

Back to the Beach Boys Concert. The day was beautiful. We were in good spirits. Georgia had food and we all brought beer. Her husband, Ephraim, was big in the forestry business. After we pulled into the driveway of their lovely home, Ephraim came out and suggested that we follow him to his place of business. He led us on a tour and told us all about the forestry business. In his office, he had a coffee table that was a giant hunk of tree. You could count the rings of the tree.

Back at their house, we talked and partied. I have never been able to do late nights. Since this night might prove to be a long one, I got a quilt from Georgia and took it outside to lie down in her yard in the sunlight. Anne and Vergie thought this was a great idea, so they also came out. I lay on the quilt looking at the filtered light through the fall trees and was reading a great spy novel. I felt so thankful at that moment. Food, beverages, an upcoming concert, Paul had not flunked out of law school, and we had great friends. There was a lot to feel thankful for.

We took off for the concert. Everybody was in great spirits. Anne's brother, Clayton, and her sister-in-law were also with us. We had barely gotten situated at the concert when the Beach Boys began to play. I was in Hog Heaven. I love the sound of the Beach Boys. They did so many great songs and I can't sing but tried anyway. Well, the crowd was way into it, and everybody was standing, singing, and dancing. Paul began to complain because the music was SO loud. None of us were really paying attention to Paul. Next thing I knew Paul was gone. He just got up and took his hips out of there. William was like, "what the f… is wrong with him?" William was "hot as a match mad." He was about to be fighting mad with all the crowd singing and hovering around all around our heads. It just seemed like Paul was ungrateful. William had gone to a lot of trouble to get those tickets. I had to be the good wife and go look for Paul. **(Although when his sister heard about his behavior, she told me, "Good wife my ass. You should have let him pout by himself and not be a buzzkill for everyone.")** There just must be some cosmic reason that I am never supposed to get to enjoy the Beach Boys in concert. Much later, when Tina Dawn was a pre- teenager, Paul went all out and got us tickets to see the Beach Boys outdoors at Memorial Stadium in Charlotte. He was not worried about the music being too loud outdoors. He even let Tina Dawn take a friend. There again, once we got situated, the Beach Boys started to play. The girls asked to get something from concessions. Time passed and they did not come back. Paul was torn up. Could they have been snatched by perverts that quickly? We began to look all over for them. Fuck me. There goes my concert again. Fortunately, they had not been kidnapped but when we finally found them, we left.

Now, back to Albany Beach Boys. The concert ended. Tensions were still high between William and Paul but everybody else was having a ball. The radio was tuned in to Beach Boys and everybody was singing. Anne's brother, Clayton, invited us all to his house which was close by. We arrived and got a beer. Clayton invited us to a rousing game of Trivial Pursuit. The teams were all geared up and excited. Paul's team went first. I have never seen this happen before or since. They won the game on the first turn. Yes, I was thankful for Paul, and he may have won Trivial Pursuit, but he did not win any popularity contest that night.

The time had come to travel to Cherryville to spend Thanksgiving with the family. It was Easy Street for me. No cooking in sight. We always ate lunch at my parents' house with that extended family. My family was very slow with all the dinners and celebrations, so Paul and I had time to wander over to Buffy's house and eventually to her daughter Bet's house. Now, at Buffy's house, just on an ordinary Sunday, she would have the best southern fried chicken ever, ham and a roast with all the sides. Her macaroni and cheese are still legendary. She made deep dish sweet potato cobbler that was "to die for." Did I mention that we drank Scotch? There were times when her small house was wall to wall people. She played soul music. We thought we were dancing but we could only just move due to the crowd just moving you about. I told you Buffy gave me heart and soul. Those were the best times. On Thanksgiving, we would go on over to Bet's because she had a house with a full basement and a bar. All the good food was there and room for fellowship and dancing. Bet had a handsome brother, Robert. Robert lived in Washington, DC. He was a concierge at a major hotel. He also loved to drink and was wild as a March hare. Every year, there would be something that Buffy forgot to bring to the celebration, but she would always ask Robert to go get her something from the grocery. Of course, he would volunteer to go and then he would never come back. Every year, like a tradition, I would say, "Big Mama, (Buffy), why did you send Robert?"

"You know he leaves, goes out partying and does not come back." Well, I guess some things never change.

We would get back to Mom's and eat there too. Then that evening, it was off to the Bell house in Stanley to feast with Paul's family. Boy, what a day of feasting.

I remember that first day after Thanksgiving, we were staying at my parent's house. (Did I tell you my mom was a little eccentric?) We were lined up to go into the kitchen for breakfast. Paul and I were hung over and Tina Dawn was tired. She has spent time at her dad's house with that set of relatives. Paul peaked into the kitchen. He came back to Tina Dawn and I and said, "is that boiled turkey and grits with sunflower seeds on top of turkey gravy?" Well, sure it is. I don't think he heard me. He was running away to barf. Now, my mama was a petite, sweet, southern belle but her cooking was a bit eccentric. Remember, I grew up there and did not realize how very odd that was. Yes, let's always be thankful for all of it. ALL OF IT!!!!!!

Christmas Gifts

The class was working away and very excited. Each child was making his own gingerbread house. We were taking cardboard, graham crackers and cake icing to make the gingerbread houses. The students were taking the cake icing to attach the graham crackers to the cardboard to make the walls and the roof. It was so clever. Once the walls were up and the graham crackers were stuck on with cake icing the decorating with candies could begin. One of my duties during this flurry of decorating was to be sure that the bus drivers would help the students get their houses home safely. It could be tricky getting on and off the bus with a gingerbread house and if other students were jealous there could be issues. So glad our drivers were good to the kids.

For some of our students Christmas was difficult, no Christmas tree, no gifts or food at home. That is why Christmas cheer was so important for our class. One of the students bragged about his beautiful tree at home. He talked about it every day but one day at lunch he kept talking in the lunchroom about eating "bad food."

I would say, "This food isn't bad," and it wasn't. Our lunch ladies made some fine food.

But then again, Maney would say, "What happens if you eat bad food?" I finally got our social worker to check on him. He not only had no Christmas tree but there was no food in the house and they were eating out of a dumpster. Of course, our social worker jumped into action and there was food. No child should ever go hungry at Christmas time or any other time.

We had our own little Christmas tree in the classroom and of course, presents were under the tree for each student. That last week we did a special class Christmas activity or craft each day. It was such a joyous time. Teachers would get gifts from the students and parents and the teachers would exchange gifts with one another. One of my teacher friends was working with students who were homebound due to medical conditions. One of the boys was unruly and would try to get out of work when she visited the home. She tried not to be too hard on him because he had anger due to being sick, home and not able to be with his friends. During one visit, he told her to get the big box under the tree with her name on it. She retrieved it but boy when she opened it, she was aghast. In the box were the ashes of the boy's Uncle Eddie. She gasped and ran. I will never forget the look on her face when she got to the office and reported on this special gift. Did you really hear me? *It was Uncle Eddie's ashes.*

I had a gift too from Maney. He told me to open it when I got home and that he hoped I would like it. I could not imagine what it would be. I got home and after supper, Paul, Tina Dawn, and I gathered in our den for the unwrapping of my present. It was a stuffed red bull. The bull was a lot like the story of the *Velveteen Rabbit* who was so loved by the child. I began to cry because I knew that it was probably his favorite toy and maybe his only toy. His card said it was to his favorite teacher. Paul immediately said, "You know after Christmas, you have to give it back." Well, of course that is what I did but I made sure that Maney knew how much his bull and I enjoyed Christmas together. Every Christmas, I have myself a good cry remembering Maney and his Christmas gift to me.

In December, at our house, Friday evenings were still a big deal. All the guys and gals came over. We still had no money, but games of darts produced some winnings. Tim had somehow gotten several bottles of wine and it was a great contest to see who a winner would be. Paul did seem to come up with a lot of wine to share at Christmas. He loves to play darts.

I remember that year that my gifts to friends and co-workers were little homemade pecan pies with a little candy cane on top. My gifts to the friends at home was homemade hot buttered rum mix. It was a gift to me from a law wife (Vergie campaigned and won to change the name of our group to law spouses!) and was a container of mix and the recipe.

Recipe: To make the hot buttered rum, you take a pound of butter (softened), a pound of powdered sugar, a pound of light or dark brown sugar, a quart of vanilla ice cream (softened), a teaspoon of cinnamon, a teaspoon of nutmeg and a quarter teaspoon of all spice and cream it until smooth. You spoon it out into airtight freezer containers and freeze. It will keep for a month. To drink, put two tablespoons in a mug with a shot of dark rum and water to fill the mug and nuke in the microwave. You are guaranteed to swoon on a cold day. My friend Louise says that was her favorite Christmas gift to this day.

The finale of the work week was the office party. I remember the office party when I was in North Carolina was held at a nice restaurant and we dressed up in our Christmas finest. Of course, it was "Dutch treat," meaning that the school did not pay for the meal, but still quite a special event. We revealed who our Secret Santa was. Early in December, each staff member would draw a name and that was our pal for the weeks leading up to Christmas. You would put little gifts in their school mailbox and receive little gifts in your box. At the end, you would get a big gift and the name of your Secret Santa. In Macon, things were a little different. First of all, the boss did not know that the name he drew was the same person who had his name. It was hilarious. He gave the same gifts back each time to the person who gave them to him. We began to call him the "Skin Flint" behind his back. He was too cheap to be a Secret Santa. Our office party that year was held at the office at the end of the workday. We all brought snacks and desserts.

We had a large bowl of punch that was delicious. *Boy was it delicious.* We slurped and drank and began to party. I felt right wild. One of the gents passed me a note that said, "*I get high on you.*" What???? I flipped out and ran away putting the note in my pocket. I am so glad that I was not pulled over driving home from the office party. I was skunk drunk. None of us (well one of us) knew that the Christmas punch was *spiked with vodka.* I got home and struggled up the stairs to our apartment. I went in the bathroom and *took that note and tore it into little pieces and threw it in the toilet.* I tried to calm down and begin to cook dinner when Paul said, "What is this? Well, bless my soul (sure wish someone had), I had forgotten to flush. He had taken each little piece out with tweezers and pieced it together. Well, sassy Annie Mae was fucked, so to speak. Paul asked a few questions but did not dwell on it. There were just no words of explanation except that we had some really good punch at the office party and all started to get a little loose lipped and fancy free. Of course, after Christmas, the office staff just knew that the two of us that worked with the behavior challenged kids had spiked the punch but low and behold, it was neither of us.

Ms. Myrtle, our special neighbor, made sure that we visited her before leaving for North Carolina. She had a rum cake made for us. We still remember that cake and it was the best one we ever had. She continued to provide us with a rum cake until she passed away. The other special gifts were for me. She gave me her costume jewelry from the twenties when she and her husband would go to a speakeasy during Prohibition. The jewelry makes me feel like a glamorous movie star each time I wear it.

The time came for us to leave Macon and arrive in Cherryville for Christmas. We spent the night on Christmas Eve with Paul's parents so we could attend the midnight candlelight service. It was beautiful and made you really feel that Christ had arrived. After the Christmas service, since it was over after midnight, it was officially Christmas. Upon arrival at the Bell household, we were able to say that it was really Christmas and that we should get to open one present. Dawn and Paul were astonished because we did get to open a present. They swore that had not happened before. That is the power of having a young child present. Tina Dawn was so excited. She had Christmas with us at Mom and Dad's, Christmas at Paul's parent's house, and Christmas at her dad's. She got Wonder Woman Underoos, a brand of children's underwear, a brown coat with fur. That is all she wore—oh yes—Underoos and a coat. Paul and I began to wonder how we would ever get all her loot in the car for the return trip to Macon.

Now, I just must tell you a story about a prior Christmas in Cherryville. The year Tina Dawn was born, Leon and I were living with his mom in her house. As usual, there was less than no money there too but we were gathered around the tree to open presents. His mom and brothers and sister were all looking at me as I opened my present. It was a Plexiglass picture cube with a cloth patch on top of its gray foam stuffing. The patch said FUCK YOU in big bold letters. I gasped, threw it down and flew out of the room crying and wailing. Yes, wailing from embarrassment and shame. My Archie Bunker husband really knew how to pour it on. The whole family was running after me yelling for me to open the bedroom door and come out. What I did not know was that inside the foam was a diamond ring. That is a Christmas I will never forget.

While in Cherryville, after spending several days of reveling with friends and family, Christmas Day had finally arrived, and we would open presents at my parent's house. Boy oh boy, I had debated about how to arrange the gift for Paul this year. Yes, the current husband, not the FUCK YOU one. I finally came up with the perfect plan. I would hock my high school class ring. I had never pawned anything before. That in and of itself was an experience. While in college, I was flat broke and needed some money, so I sold my flute and piccolo to a high school friend rather than go with the pawn shop experience. Nevertheless, I got brave and went to the pawn shop and got the needed bucks and bought Paul a briefcase. He was going to be a lawyer. A lawyer needs to have a briefcase. Paul had also debated about how to arrange to get me the perfect gift. He pawned his class ring and bought me a flute at the pawnshop. Have you ever read "The Gift of the Magi?" We had the most perfect Christmas ever.

The Joys of Being Mom

———◆———

In Macon, Tina Dawn was a minority and was picked on daily. This was hard for a child who was only eight years old. If she wore a necklace, they would pull it off her neck. Some of the kids would even chase her down the street as she was going home. It was hard on a little kid.

What was there to do in Macon in winter? A lot. Our Tina Dawn was born cheering. No lie. She could talk before she could walk. Seriously. Was her first word Mom or Dad? No, it was "cookie." She was so cute, and my brother loved to give her cookies and make her talk. She was a poster child for wanting children.

Once she found out that there would be cheerleading for the little boys' recreational football team, she was so there. Well, of course they loved her. It did not matter that she was a minority. To have a tiny blond in the lineup was just fine with the cheerleading coach. And the cheerleading coach decided that I needed to be her assistant coach. My, oh my. I had a brief stint as cheerleader but was not in the league of our coach. It was helpful to her to have someone to take charge if she was late or had to be absent. We did such famous cheers as "Hey Kung Fu, You Know We're After You" with karate kicks. They were pretty cute. Our little boys were undefeated and made it to the Super Bowl. It was a big deal. They played the game in one of the big high school stadiums. Our girls and boys were so excited. Just think they were so young, eight to ten, and felt like they had made it to the big time. At the same time, we were getting ready for the big game, Tina Dawn won a Bibb County art contest representing her school. We were so proud of her. They were having a big ceremony also at the main library for the winners. You guessed it. Both celebrations were on the same day. Paul and I had to divide and conquer. Well, he got to go to the Super Bowl, and I got to go to the library alone. Tina Dawn's principal was there to greet me. When Tina Dawn's name was called, I proudly went forward and onto the stage to accept the award for her. I never expected that the award would be a gerbil in a cage with food and all donated by a local pet store. A gerbil!!!!! Oh my, thank you. I could not believe this. I so wanted to let the gerbil go on the way home and get her some candy or something but no, I was the good mother. Paul and Tina Dawn came in carrying on. Their team won the game and ended the year undefeated. I got a plaque and Tina Dawn got a trophy. Boy, were they surprised when I introduced a gerbil to our celebration. Well, Tina Dawn was delighted. She had wanted a pet and living in an apartment, I guess he could be welcomed into our humble home. Since he was an art award, he was named Van Gogh. What a glorious day at our house.

It was time to celebrate Tina Dawn's success with our buddies. We all met at the Grey Goose, a local bar and restaurant, for goose burgers. What is a goose burger, you might ask? It is a most delicious hamburger cooked on an old grill with all the trimmings. To wash it down with a cold beer was just what we needed. Our queen for a day, Tina Dawn got a Shirley Temple to go with her burger. The day would have been perfect, except that while in the parking lot, William ran over Paul's foot and while we screamed, he backed over it again. Fortunately, Paul is a tough one, and his foot was not broken. It was just bruised like William's ego.

Macon was not famous for winter weather. I was just blown away when we did not have school one day because it was too cold for the students to be out at the bus stop. What the Hell? Well, OK, I could enjoy a "cold day" at home too. I could not believe it one day when I was hard at work, and it began to snow like crazy. I mean crazy; that was the way my co-workers were acting. In North Carolina we had a few bouts of freezing weather and a couple snow storms a year but Macon was just wild with snow fever. When I tried to drive down Vineville Avenue, it was bumper to bumper traffic. I was afraid that I would run out of gas before I got home. Once I got home, it was serious play time. Paul and I had bought cross-country skis. I know you are reading and thinking, oh yes, they had less than no money and here they were with cross-country skis. Before our sojourn to Macon, this backpacking store in Charlotte was going out of business. We knew one of the owners and he was practically giving us stuff. We got the skis, ski poles, a pair of Vask boots, and a number of other things. We did not have a lot of opportunities to get to use the skis. We put those skis on and skied down Vineville Avenue. It was such a hoot. It may be that no one had ever skied down Vineville before or since. Our picture skiing down Vineville was printed in the local paper.

Now, I am no skier. Cross-country is a little easier for me than downhill skiing. Once while in college at Gardner Webb I had the opportunity to take a course in skiing. You went for a weekend during Christmas break and actually took the whole course and got a grade. I was a PE major at that time, so skiing made sense. One of the girls who was scheduled to go had a death in the family and was about to cancel when me and my crazy high school friend, Jean, decided that she could go in Susan's place. We had such a wicked time. This will sound like such bull shit, but I swear it is the truth that the famous Olympic skier John Claude Keely was teaching the course at the French Swiss Ski College at Appalachian State in Boone, North Carolina. I will never forget seeing my friend Jean skiing down the slope in her blue and white polka dotted bibs. John Claude had the class lined up and was teaching us a skill when Jean skied over all our skis and knocked the whole class down. Lots of us students were all staying together, and

I do not know how many of us were actually sleeping in the same bed.

At one point during this college ski adventure, Jean and I went out to do some New Year's Eve celebrations back in Cherryville. Yes, we drove down the mountain from Boone and drove back to Cherryville. Why? You might ask. Yes, we were crazy party girls in Boone so why not back in our old hometown of Cherryville. My parents were out of town and Jean, and I decided we could have a little party at the empty house. Well, one of my ex-husband's aunts started the evening by spilling a whole bottle of booze all over the place. Buffy, my precious nanny, was trying to help us clean up when two of the guys started to get into a knife fight. Jean and I thought this was a formal party and my ex and his crew showed up in jeans and were raising hell. The police finally had to be called to end the party. Here we were in our formal dresses trying to clean and disinfect my parents' house in a flash. Buffy was directing our efforts because, yes, you guessed it, we had to head back from Cherryville up the mountain to Boone to complete our skiing class!!!!

Jean and I were careening back up the road into Boone and were about to pee in our pants. We really had to go. We pulled into a liquor store parking lot. It was the wee hours of the morning and dark as a tomb as we pulled down our britches and let it go. Next thing we knew there were blue lights flashing and oh yes there were the police. We snatched those britches back up just as the po po were accusing us of trying to rob the liquor store. I told them that we stopped there to pee and that one of them was standing in a puddle of proof. He jumped back and shook off his shoe. Thankfully they let us go and we sang the Fuck Fuck chorus as we made our way back to the bed full of folks at App State. We had a blast and Susan got a C in the skiing class and was never there.

Back from my young adult winter crazy to Tina Dawn's busy winter in Macon. She also regularly attended ballet classes. The ballet instructor was superb. She was strict and really did carry a stick. She insisted on perfection and developed good dancers. Tina Dawn learned to dance and is a good dancer to this day. Those skills helped her also as she became a college cheerleader later. The highlight of the ballet season in Macon was the December presentation of the Nutcracker. Tina Dawn had several parts: as one of the little girls and as a soldier. She had beautiful costumes, and they practiced many hours to put on this performance at the Macon Opera House. The Grand Opera House, also known as the Grand, was built in 1884. It has been a vaudeville house, a movie palace and has hosted numerous famous performers. It has been restored and renovated and is managed by Mercer University.

The real kicker was that a ballet dancer from Russia was brought in to dance the lead. He was amazing to watch. All our relatives came to Macon to see the performance. Maw Maw, my ex's mother (Tina Dawn's grandmother) came and stayed with us. My co-workers found it amusing that my ex-mother-in-law was staying with us but all of us loved her. It was not a problem for Paul at all. He loved her too. Now the ex and the other relatives stayed in a motel. My mother and father thought this was the greatest thing. They bought Tina Dawn, a Sugarplum Fairy doll that was beautiful. They bought us beautiful ceramic nutcracker ornaments. Even now, I love to cherish those memories as I put those ornaments on the tree each year. The performance was fantastic, and Tina Dawn felt like a star. The one thing she kept saying about the rehearsals and the performances was that the Russian dancer, who had an ass almost as good as Baryshnikov (I would love to just bite that ass.) Anyway, she said he could sling some sweat as he danced about the stage.

It seems like, as a mom, we are so busy running from home to work to pick up the child at all their events, and so forth winter, summer, spring, and fall. It is such a major labor of love. It is a time in our lives that goes by way too fast.

Woody and Professional Learning

Wow, returning from Christmas was special for me at work. No longer was I shunned in the lounge; everybody was glad to see me. What happened? I felt like I was a welcome grain of salt. It was like they were welcoming a BFF, Best Friend Forever. I am not kidding. There would be no more crying at night in our apartment on Vineville Avenue. The teachers wanted me to lead an aerobics workshop for them after school a couple of days a week. They even gave me a nickname "Cut." My teacher assistant, Betty Mae, had the nickname "Cut," and her BFF Royce had the nickname "Cut," so we were known as "Cut," "Cut," and "Cut." I was so glad to feel welcome in the "pepper shaker."

It was such a wonderful time for me. I got called to the office one day. I had a phone call from a guy at the central office. He said that I had been nominated for the Council for Exceptional Children Teacher of the Year

Award. I said, "Sure I have. Who are you and how did my husband talk you into this dirty trick?"

You see, back in Belmont, North Carolina, I got called to the office that one of my students' parents needed to speak to me and left his name and number. When I called, it was the funeral home and the man was a dead body. Paul thought that was the funniest thing. So did the staff at my school. Me, not so much. Well, the man on the other end of the phone in Macon said, "I don't know what you are talking about. This is no joke. You are well respected in the district and a nomination came in for you."

Then he gave me information about the upcoming banquet. I was too excited to breathe. I wore my favorite dress for the banquet. It was a red 1940's style dress that seemed to be my "good luck dress."

I had the privilege back in North Carolina to get to be a hair style model in a hair style competition in Charlotte. The hairdresser and I had so much fun preparing for the competition. My mom took the hairdresser and me shopping to pick out the dress from Montaldo's dress shop in Charlotte. My hair style was 1940s with a big white feather coming out of the rolled and plaited upswept hairdo that had a basket weave in the back. The dress was a perfect vintage-look 40s red dress. Mom and a best friend of hers accompanied us to the competition. When they called the hairdresser's name that he had won first place, I leaped out of my seat and ran to the award podium like I had won. It was so ridiculous. I jumped up so fast that the feather flew out of my hair. The audience and judges were stunned but my hairdresser was delighted and reached down and put that feather back in my hair. He let me help him receive the trophy and he really did need me. Honest to Pete, that trophy was almost as big as me. I loved that dress so much. I wore it until it literally fell apart. Yes, that was my "Good Luck Dress."

I guess it was also a "good luck dress again" because I won the Teacher of the Year Award at the reception in Macon. The beautiful trophy with the CEC seal and a fountain pen made me feel special. It made my parents proud too. My dad wrote me a letter to congratulate me that I will keep forever.

When I went on stage to get the award, there was a green plastic snake wrapped around it and I just played dumb and smiled and made an ordinary acceptance speech. Why the snake? This all goes back to a professional learning event in a high school auditorium in Macon. I have always loved to be part of practical jokes. Not jokes that potentially hurt anyone but things that I think are funny. Now Paul frequently says, "You think you are funny, but you are not." This may qualify as one of those times. The guy, Rory, who was now teaching my former behavior support class in Macon was sitting beside me and we were listening to the speaker during the professional learning event. The auditorium was full of teachers getting advice on how to become even better teachers. Truthfully, I do not remember the topic that was being presented that day. Rory leaned over and asked if I would like to walk outside to his car to see his pet python named Woody. Sure. Out we went. Woody, indeed, was in his car in a big cage. He got Woody out and said that we should carry Woody back into the auditorium with us. Sure. It took both of us to carry Woody to the school auditorium. He was over six feet long and as big around as my thigh. Rory raised mice just to feed Woody and said that Woody had been very bad once and ate a cat. As we got to the door, Rory put Woody around his neck and proceeded inside. When we got back to our seats (so glad the audience was enthralled with the speaker) Rory put Woody down on the floor. The floor was cold, and Woody began to crawl toward the front of the auditorium. Oh, hello he was slithering between people's feet, and they did not even know. Rory and I were about to croak. The speaker ended and audience members began to make their way up to speak to the presenter. A lady looked down and saw Woody and screamed "SNAKE." The audience began to run for the doors, crawling over each other, trying to get away. It was sheer, unadulterated madness. Rory began to fear for Woody and ran down and swooped him up and we ran out the stage doors, thankfully making a hasty getaway.

When April Fool's Day rolled around that year, Rory and I had the bright idea of putting Woody in the special education director's office. We met at the central office that morning and got Woody out. As we went into the boss's office area, the secretary and those standing around scattered. I had made a little cartoon sign to put on the boss's door, BEWARE OF THE APRIL FOOL. We laid Woody out on the credenza and got into the closet. The boss came in and opened the door and immediately went back out to get coffee and left the door open. Oh, my.... Those who had scattered continued to make themselves real scarce. Rory and I were absolutely hysterical. We were hugging on each other in that closet laughing, crying and snotting. Finally, after what seemed like an eternity, the boss came back in and went to his desk. He began to yell. Someone, Anyone, come on. Rory and I ventured out of the closet. He told us to take Woody and that Woody better never show up again at any office, school, professional learning activity or any school event, period or that Rory and I would be looking for other gainful employment. We did get Woody and vacate but we laughed all the way out to the car. What an absolute hoot.

    I guess the third time is the charm. It was the last day of school and we on the "dark side" were having our staff meeting in the conference room. The boss told me there was a call from one of my schools that I needed to leave post haste and go help with an immediate crisis in the parking lot there. I was like, "Oh Hell. Of course, someone must act a pure fool on the last day of school, and it just has to be me that gets the privilege of putting out the fire." I was thinking all these loving thoughts as I proceeded to get my purse and go out the door.

    As I was leaving, not in a happy way, to break up a fracas on the last day of school, I heard "Bell," and went back. OK, this is your April Fool. There is no crisis at the school, come in and sit back down. Yes, there again, he had me. Some pranks just keep on giving. Many years later, when we located back in North Carolina, the special education director, yes in North Carolina, said that she better never have a snake in her office. How she knew, I have no idea.

The Barrel Cabins

———◆———

William, Anne, Paul, Tina Dawn, and I came up with a great idea during one of our Friday after hours soirees at the Bell abode. We decided that we should do a little vacation for Valentines' Day and stay in Helen, Georgia. Helen is a small Bavarian town in the Georgia Mountains. It has waterfalls, beautiful scenic views, shopping, beer, beer steins and German food. The town started as a home to the Cherokee Indians, then it became home to the European settlers and finally lovers of its German Bavarian theme since the 1960s. It is a little village with little Bavarian decorated houses. It is so damn cute. We stayed in a cabin in Unicoi State Park that was a big wooden barrel on stilts. It looked like a whiskey barrel. The bathtub was so tiny with the barrel roof that Tina Dawn was the only one that could stand up in the shower in the bathtub. Tina Dawn asked, "How are the grown-ups going to wash themselves?" Speaking of damn cute; but how William, Paul, Anne, Tina Dawn, and I fit in that tiny barrel cabin remains to be seen. Sleeping in a bed like crows on a fence piled in like cordwood. I guess we just really wanted a vacation.

There were all kinds of things to do there. We shopped at all the little stores. Of course, Tina Dawn found those dollar grab bags just like the ones my parents bought her in Gatlinburg, so she was as happy as a little pig in slop. We went into a shop called Keiser Bill's. We all got into a conversation with Old Keiser Bill. He talked about how we were young people and needed to be concerned about our health and Lord knows that was so true. Here we were guzzling all this beer and eating pretzels and German food. Keiser Bill, The Proprietor went on to elaborate (yes this was a painstakingly long sermon). He told us how he preserved his health and lived to be a crusty old dude. He said that the secret to his long abundant life was colonics. Now, I am from Cherryville, NC and don't know nothing about no colonics. Everybody was giving me the stink eye. They just knew I was going to have to say something. Of course, I asked, "Sir, what is colonics?" He said that you go to the spa. Now, it is nothing like a back rub or a foot scrub. Oh no, no, no, why they stick a pipe up your ass and proceed to give you an enema and get all the shit out of your ass and colon and somehow that is supposed to help you live longer. It might help me live longer, but I will just stick with the old-fashioned back rub if ever in a spa. Now, if you go to Helen in 2024, and the proprietor at Keiser Bill's is still alive, and you know he probably is, he will proceed to tell you all about colonics. After that period of enlightenment, Paul and William decided to splurge and bought beer steins. I will always remember William's stein. It was a wild boar with these adorable little white tusks. I loved it and still love it to this day. I loved it so damn much that I don't even remember what kind of stein Paul bought. Now, Anne and I were all wrapped up into the jewelry. I tried on this ring and Anne said the famous and often used expression, "are you going to buy it? Because if you are not, I am." It was an amethyst ring that had gold and silver with a design that sort of looks like a sperm. Anyway, yes, contemporary and weird but a lovely splurge just the same. We were spending money like drunken sailors and having a momentary lapse in judgment, but oh, what sheer fun. We had been filling our bellies swilling that German beer and there is nothing really like drunk shopping. It will cure what ails you. We also ate sausages with kraut in the German fashion. We just wandered around and had a blast.

Now one of the great things about the barrel cabin was the nighttime. What are you going to do? It was quiet, view the mountains, have a few more beers. Well, we played games. We took games with us. Most of the games involved decks of cards. That little kitchen table was the perfect place for games. We grown-ups sat at the table and Tina Dawn just stood up in her spot behind Paul and Annie Mae. One of the games that we played was Spoons.

If you have not played this game, you must learn how: You will need spoons and a deck of cards.

Count your players. In the middle of the table, place however many spoons is one less than the number of players you have. For example, if you're playing with 6 people, use 5 spoons.

Shuffle the cards and deal 4 to each person. Have the dealer keep the deck next to them.

Have everyone take one of their cards and discard it to their left simultaneously. The person to the right of the dealer puts one of their cards down on the table to start the discard pile, while the dealer picks up a new card.

You do not have to exchange cards with the card you are given, if you do not want to. Instead, just pass the card you received on to the player to your left. Repeat this process of everyone passing to the left. Each round the dealer should pick up a new card and the person to their right should add to the discard pile, so as to have a continuous growth of new cards.

All players continue to circulate cards. It usually goes pretty quickly and can be tough to keep track of! This is intentional and makes the game more fun.

The first person to have 4 of a kind like 4 aces or 4 7s, etc., has to yell and pick up a spoon. Following this, all other players need to do the same, with the slowest person left without a spoon and out of the game. You are tense and start to reach for the spoon but if you pick up a spoon before you have the 4 of a kind, you are out.

Usually, William or Paul would try to be sneaky and just slip a spoon with no one realizing it. The game gets crazy. At the point you reach in to grab the spoon, one person is left out.

The Paul/William tactic – you grab the spoon with the handle down knocking the other spoons off the table. The other players fall to the floor and fight over the spoons under the table.

Tina Dawn always talks about this Spoons Game as a memory anytime we discuss our life in Macon because at one point, Paul and William (neither of them are lightweights) both leaped onto the table to grab spoons and oh yes, Hell yes, broke down the damn table. We were lucky that no one had a serious game injury.

Later, after our Macon law school lifetime ended, we went back to Helen Georgia to see those barrel cabins. We, to this day, cannot figure out how our group fit into a cabin. Well, maybe those cabins just had shrunk over time! I don't think we had expanded as much as those cabins had shrunk.

The Cherry Blossom Festival

———◆———

Macon was a beautiful city that came alive in the spring with those beautiful cherry blossoms. We heard that there was going to be a festival with food vendors, art work, crafts for sale, a stage with music and a costume contest. This sounded just crazy. We had told people all about the festival and were going to go with William and Anne and Vergie and Tim and other assorted law school buddies who would meet there at the festival site. After hearing that crazy spring fever fun was possible, Dawn, Paul's sister, and Jimmy, Dawn's significant other, also did the drive in from North Carolina to join us all for the festival.

The festival takes place annually in Carolyn Crayton Park in Macon, Georgia. Macon seems to turn pink with over 350,000 Yoshino cherry trees in bloom. There are 10 days of fun and frivolity. The first festival took place in 1982. It had a humble beginning but now is one of the top festival events in the south. I believe that since our crew was at that very first festival that must be the reason it was such a huge success. Well, maybe.

Costume, costume, well Annie Mae will use any excuse to wear a costume. I had this great Wonder Woman costume and voila here I go. After drinking copious amounts of beer and looking at all the food and shopping, it was time for the costume contest. I had to go get my name in and receive a number to get in the lineup. When it was my turn, why I pranced like a pony up on that great stage and showed out as Wonder Woman. Well, William, for his costume he had a red bandana that he wrapped around his head and he was right there in the middle of Macon saying "Lordy, Lordy, Miss Scarlet, I don't know nothing about birthing no babies." We all were aghast. Politically correct. Not. We all held him back saying that night was not a good night to be murdered at the festival. So no thank God Hell no we did not let William make his way to the stage.

So, I am still showing out as Wonder Woman. Did anyone else in our crew have on a costume? No. but that did not stop or deter my fun in any way. I walked up to a vendor who was selling this awesome brass jewelry that was actually in my price range. I picked out a ring with a man and woman being romantic and with their hands on each other's privates. How cool. I bought it right quick before anyone else could. I loved it and proudly put it on my finger right then. *I needed the brass ring!* This man and woman enjoying each other intertwined. I was walking around staring at the ring just thinking what a happy night. *This would really commemorate my mischief in Macon.* We were all having the best time. We continued to walk around and finally had to take our hips to the house.

The crew descended on our humble home and we began our after party. The plan was to drink and play darts. As I continued to show off my brass ring, Dawn and Jimmy began to mutter. "What's that you say?" "Well, take off that ring." "We want to see it up close and personal." I did and low and behold, Jimmy gasped. *"Why that is two men."*

"Oh SNAP, surely not."

"Give it back, let me see."

I was arguing, *"See that one has a little bun on the back of her head. She is a woman."*

Then the more they groaned and the more I looked at it...

"Well damn if it ain't."

"Who is sober enough to drive me back to that festival?" I actually do not remember who went back with me but we w*ent Hell for leather* back to the Cherry Blossom Festival. We went back to the brass booth. I proceeded to tell the jewelry maker what my friends and relatives said about my ring. They said that it was two men intertwined holding each other's privates. The artist said that it was a man and a woman intertwined holding wine glasses. I told him right there and then making a bit of a spectacle of myself that one of the wine glasses had to go. He said that my friends were perverts and I said, *"Yes, but they are still my friends, cut it off."* He proceeded to work his magic and castrated my ring. I put it back on and proudly went back home. To me, romance is romance and the ring could have been fine with me. Now, my friends and relatives were a bit excessive in their judgment, but I do love them and that ring!

Now, I not only had a ring to commemorate my mischief in Macon, but a story to go with it. Dawn, Paul's sister, and Jimmy were so much fun. They did not visit Macon often. We got to show them sites like the law school and downtown Macon. They really enjoyed our weekend.

Now, readers, you are not going to believe this shit. My picture as Wonder Woman was a foot tall in the Macon newspaper. I look like thunder thighs. When I got to work, that picture showed up all over the place. Talk about showing out. I felt right famous.

Colder than a Witch's Tit

———◆———

Well, I just want to talk about how spring fever was alive and well in Macon, Georgia. We all decided that our whole crew would go camping at Stone Mountain, Georgia. That was William, Anne, Vergie, Tim, Tina Dawn, Paul and I and Paul's sister Dawn and Jimmy. It was special for the only child in the crew, Tina Dawn, to get to go with us. If you have ever camped, you know how hard it is to get ready for the trip. You must get out all the stuff and Paul always had to check it all out to make absolutely sure that all was in order. You have to have the meals figured out to know who is bringing what. We were very excited and took off to Stone Mountain. When we got to the campground, we set up our camp site on the peninsula at the lake. We camped in the same area so that we could hang out as a group, eat together at night, and bond at the fire. The fire is the major event for Anne. That girl is somewhat of a pyromaniac when it comes to campfires. She is the one getting wood and making all of us help look for wood. The fact that there were not a lot of tents or campers should have raised questions. Now, in retrospect, we should have wondered why. The thing that we did not count on was how COLD it was. We were thinking "spring" break, but the weather was thinking "winter." It was so COLD. Another thing we should have thought of was how the wind would feel and sound coming off the lake. Oh my, it felt like needles poking in your skin and the howling sound reminded me of a horror movie that has no survivors making you ask yourself who in Hell would camp in this weather?

We got up the next morning and huddled around the campfire drinking coffee and saying wow this just sucks. The adults decided to warm up by drinking liquor. Yes, I do mean "day drinking." What do you do when you get cold? Well, you drink. We had our scurvy medicine and flasks of Jack Daniels; I rarely ever go camping without my best buddy Jack. Instead of sitting at the camp site enjoying the nice "spring" weather, we just rode around in the car looking for places that would be warm. We even went into bathrooms to warm ourselves using the hand dryers. I am not shitting you. I am serious as a heart attack. It was seriously cold and there was little Tina Dawn. But we carried on and made it till campfire time in the evening when we hung out, drank more, and told stories. Now let me tell you about sleeping when it's colder than a well digger's ass in Montana. YOU DON'T! You have this mummy bag that's supposed to keep you nice and warm but not so much.

So, then it became Easter Sunday, and the deal was that there was an Easter Sunrise Service at the top of Stone Mountain. You heard me, you had to climb to the top of Stone Mountain before sunrise. Well, I, of course, could not wait to do that and Anne could not wait to do that and neither could Tim and Vergie. The rest of the crew, except for Tim, Vergie, Anne, and Annie Mae was like, "Fuck no. See you when you get back, if you get back. We can have breakfast when we get back. You are crazy people. You will freeze your asses off."

I don't even know how Anne and I managed to get up without waking everyone else up and putting on, oh yes, every bit of clothes we had. We looked like giant puff balls in hiking boots. We began the stumble up the mountain. Vergie and Tim had gone on ahead of us. There were others braving the cold winding our way to the top. The wind felt like it would blow us right off the mountain. That would sure be an ugly obituary. Blown off Stone Mountain on Easter Sunday. At one point, Anne and I were passing a large furry white dog and our eyes met. We both looked at each other and thought about just lying under that dog but we pressed onward. I was so cold and afraid that I would topple off the mountain just from being frozen. It was colder than a witches' tit in a brass brassiere, for real. I will tell you that when the sun rose over Stone Mountain on Easter Sunday with people singing, "Jesus Christ is risen today," I cried a river. It was such a beautiful experience. All we both could do was cry. The light and the fullness of nature not to mention the silence with hundreds of people on the mountain so connected and so grounded that it was hard to describe the fullness of it. We felt like we were in the presence of God. And hell yes, it was worth the cold hike up the mountain. Well, we made it down the mountain and ate our big breakfast.

It was time for the crew to "break camp" and get ready to head home. Now, boys will be boys. There was William over trying to take his tent down. Now, William is a big guy, but he has no ass. His pants were falling around his ankles and Tim, Jimmy and Paul lowered the tent down all around him. He had on red long handle underwear but OMG, the flap was open. Tina Dawn was hysterical. She had seen the crack of William's ass so many times growing up. It was so damn funny. We all were dying laughing and poor William was laughing too and saying, "Guys, Guys."

Yes, leaving a fun vacation is always a little melancholy. Everyone was going back to school and work. But oh no, not Annie Mae. All I had to do was get home and do an unpack and repack because I was heading to the Council for Exceptional Children's Conference in Washington, DC. I had to unpack and repack in time for Paul to drive us wild women to Atlanta to hop on board the Amtrak train. Right before Easter break, all my teacher friends knew that I did not have much money for this trip. Paul tried to scrape together some funds and I was doing a presentation. There was little school system money for my travel, registration, hotel, and food. I was sharing a room with "Hut" and we were going on the train to save money. But right before I left the school the last day prior to the holidays there was a little Easter basket in my box at work with plastic eggs and money in them. I was blown away. That was so sweet and now I was set! My buddies had come through for me. I had greenbacks for DC. Paul got us to the train on time. I just thought the train was wonderful. We had these big recliners to sleep in. Remember, I don't leave home without my favorite liquor, Jack Daniels, and I had books to read. It turned out that Easter had been a big old time for the Amtrak, and they were running out of food and booze. I was even popular with strangers on the train, me and my Jack Daniels. Eating sandwiches, drinking, and reading in my recliner, I was sawing some zs quickly. Well, "Hut," and the girls jumped up in the middle of the night yelling, "Annie Mae, get up get up, you are there." Well, Hell the train had stopped in Gastonia, NC close to my hometown of Cherryville. Those hussies woke me up for the hell of it. If you have ever ridden the train, it stops in every town. It was a slow ride to DC. Lucky me, I went right back to sleep but those poor women were up all night. We finally made it to DC. Once we got our suitcases off the train, there was "Hut." "We are buying plane tickets and never riding that train again." Not so fast. Where is all that money coming from? Of course, we just kept on walking and got our ride to the hotel.

I had only been to Washington, DC, at the age of 9 with all my cousins. I did not remember how totally awesome Washington, DC, is. We were good stewards of the taxpayers' money and did attend our sessions. But we also saw the city. We loved the Smithsonian and saw all kinds of exhibits and gorgeous art works. We saw the space museum and loved walking in the mall area of the city.

While at the conference, we were also collecting stickers from all the vendors that were selling books and materials. In the process, we received a valuable invitation to a huge party hosted by the Division of the Morally Impaired, DMI. The CEC conference is divided into real divisions standing for the various disabilities one might have. For example, I was a member of CCBD. Council for Children with Behavior Disorders. These crazy guys had made up DMI and even collected dues to have a hotel suite and host this bash at every national conference. We girls got all dolled up and here we went. Now, the deal is, that if you do something lewd and lascivious, you get a t-shirt from DMI. The t-shirt this year had the Washington monument in the center with cherry blossoms and DMI in the middle. Now, I know I have a dirty mind, but hey, the nation has a phallic symbol, The Washington Monument. To me, it looks like a giant dildo. The slogan on the shirt was "Sorry You Could Not Be First, but You Could Be Next." I had to have that shirt. What to do? What to do? The party was in full swing with music and an open bar and a bathtub full of bottles of champagne. I had on my gold spandex pants (some might have whispered the words, camel toe) but what the hell. I also had on an off one shoulder top to match. Well, down just that one strap and Annie Mae was topless, yes, she was. The cab ride back to the hotel was an adventure also. The cab driver did not speak very good English and here it was the middle of the night and he took us to Virginia and tried to let us out instead of to Maryland, where we were staying. We were squealing and screaming and carrying on because my presentation was first thing in the morning.

Well, the guys and gals from Macon assisted me with my presentation. It was about using videos to change behavior. I called the presentation, "Seeing is Believing." I videotaped my class, with parental permission, of course. The students were able to see their behavior in action. During parent conferences, the parents could view how their child performed in a classroom situation. The presentation went well. Later, I was able to publish an article about this in the journal, *Teaching Exceptional Children*, spring 1995, "Using videotape to Communicate with Parents of Students with Severe Disabilities." Well, that was our last day. All good spring breaks must eventually come to an end. What a terrific pair of trips. At least in DC, it was not as "cold as a witch's tit." We had lovely spring weather, cherry blossoms, and a super time with only a small amount of mischief.

Once we got back to Atlanta, I was wearing those camel toe spandex pants and my DMI t-shirt. Paul immediately noticed the t-shirt and said, "I just don't want to know," and of course my girlfriends know that whatever happens at DMI stays at DMI.

The Magic Kids

I know you remember that Paul performed magic tricks on our first date. No, he was not naked and we were not in bed... yet.

After we married, he continued to suggest that I use magic to build the self-esteem of my students. He enjoyed magic as a hobby and had used magic successfully, not only on that first date and in bed, but also to get student's attention when he was a social worker.

Magic transports us into the land of make-believe where the magician is master. A truly baffling illusion excites us. It makes us wonder: "How was it done? Can I do it myself?" Imagine a child's emotions when the child achieves the ability to inspire this awe and curiosity in their classmates, friends, and family.

My first of many of my Magic Kids were my students in Macon. This became the after Christmas project. First, they had to take the Magician's Oath. You can only teach an illusion if you are teaching it to another magician. I would teach a trick on Monday during Class Meeting. The students would have until Friday to practice the trick on each other or to perform it in front of the mirror. There was no pressure. They would do that during their free time if they liked the trick and wanted to learn it. Some tricks are more complicated than others. Then on Friday, the ones that felt proficient would perform it for The Group. I would remind the other students to practice being a good audience so they would have a good audience when they decided to perform a magic trick. We continued in that pattern until the class had mastered enough to put on a magic show.

Another positive aspect of learning magic tricks was all the organizational and academic skills that go into learning a magic trick. You must know how to "load" the trick so the illusion will work. You must remember all the steps to perform the trick in order while saying something to the audience that might be misdirection. We took a cart and Betty Mae put cloth around it on three sides so we could have our tricks loaded on the shelves and use the top of the cart like our stage to perform from. The more proficient students were the magicians, and the more timid students were the assistants. Part of performing a magic trick is the "patter" or speech that goes along with it. Some of the students just were not ready for that yet. We practiced our show until we felt we were READY. I got the other teachers to sign up for times for The Magic Kids to perform a magic show for their class.

Imagine, if you can, that you are sitting in a fourth-grade class. A teacher and a band of costumed performers enter. They are pushing a cart that is covered in black and inscribed with stars and magic symbols. A magic wand is lying on top of the cart. Then softly, the beginning of the classical music Shahrazad begins to play. The music at the beginning is dramatic. The teacher with the performers starts to narrate the story of "Aladdin." This is one of the tales from 1001 Arabian nights. It is also an animated movie. As she speaks of a dark cave, a student magician comes forward, picks up the magic wand and says, "There was smoke and fire in the cave!" He waves the wand, and a fireball shoots out toward the ceiling. The teacher says, "I would like to present The Magic Kids and their interpretation of 'Aladdin.'"

Needless to say, we were a success. Word traveled and the classes were so excited to see us. It did a lot to change the image of my students in their eyes. I was able to have Magic Kids at two schools in Macon. The students in the second school were very smart and some even gifted. One of those students was the only student I had to this day who could do the billiard ball routine and he learned to juggle. He was inspiring to me. I could not do the billiard ball trick or juggle, but I just made them available for him and he taught himself. That group did a great rendition of Aladdin.

You may be asking yourself why these smart, savvy students were in my other class for behaviorally challenged students. They all had been victims of trauma.

My billiard ball fellow was in a group that I took to camp. You have already heard some of these crazy camp stories. This is still shocking to me. When we went to the lake area, he took off his shirt to swim. One of the camp counselors called me over. He had welt marks all over his back. We were required by law to call this into social services. He had been beaten by his mom with a small belt. I had wondered what the source of his anger was.

This second class of mine was visited by a friend who was a good amateur magician that performed regularly for parties and events. (You will also hear about him in another excerpt, The Rabbit is Rich). He gave my students some critiques, but he was significantly impressed with their magic show.

At a meeting of teachers of exceptional children, I mentioned what we were doing. After that, the Very Special Arts Festival planner contacted me to see if my class would do a performance during the festival at Central City Park in Macon.

Central City Park (now called Carolyn Crayton Park) is home to Macon's historic Luther Williams Field, the heart of Cherry Blossom Festival events, and the original home of the Georgia State Fair, Carolyn Crayton Park was Macon's first and largest public park.

Historic Luther Williams Field has also served as a film location for *Trouble with the Curve* starring Clint

Eastwood and Amy Adams. (Historical information from the Central City Park website).

The Magic Kids performed exceptionally well at this outdoor event. I only had to introduce them. They did the rest. You have already heard about a camp incident with my lead off magician, Dick. I had to eat with him each day. One day, he asked me what I was going to be when I grew up. I spurted, sputtered, and said, "I am being it. I am doing it." He did show great social skills as he performed The Mind Reader. It uses magic terms such as Force, One Ahead, and Misdirection. This is difficult particularly in front of an audience that was much bigger than the audience in a classroom. I was amazed at his performance because I must admit I was a little nervous. Betty Mae and I were so proud of our students. There were people from our school also in the audience who gave us rave reviews. This event was a self-esteem booster for all of us. We received a beautiful picture from the Very Special Arts Committee to commemorate our fine performance.

Now, you can be a Mind Reader too but only if you take the Magician's Oath and only reveal the secret to another aspiring magician.

The magician tells the audience that he can read minds. He asks for an audience volunteer who has money in his pocket. The magician tells the volunteer to keep his hand on the money in his pocket and not show the money. The magician feels the volunteer's head to "read his mind" and says, "I will write on this blank slip of paper the amount of money in your pocket, and I will label this Test A." The volunteer then shows the money to the magician and the audience. The volunteer takes a bow and sits down. (The magician really writes Test C on the slip and draws a circle and puts the slip in the magic hat).

The second volunteer is called up to gather or produce 3 objects from around them or from a purse, etc. After showing the objects to the audience, the volunteer is supposed to concentrate on one of the objects while the magician "reads his mind." Then the magician writes the name of the object and labels the slip Test B (the magician is really writing Test A and the amount of money). The magician asks the volunteer which object he was concentrating on and tells the audience to remember the object.

The third volunteer is called up. The magician shows the audience that he has three shapes, a square, a circle, and a triangle. He will predict the shape the volunteer will pick before he picks it. He "reads the volunteer's mind" and writes the shape on a slip of paper labeled Test C (he is really writing the object and labeling it Test B). The magician then asks the volunteer to choose a shape. Put the circle in the middle because it is most often chosen. If the volunteer chooses a different one, then say we don't need that one. Then if he chooses circle, you don't need the other one, etc. You force them to choose the circle.

The magician chooses a fourth volunteer to read the slips from the magic hat beginning with Test A, etc. Magically, The Mind Reader has read the minds and made the correct predictions. During the ensuing thunderous applause, the magician thanks the last volunteer and asked all the volunteers to stand, and they all bow together.

The Mind Reader is my personal favorite. It mystifies audiences and requires no expense and little preparation.

If you want to explore magic as a teacher further, you can read my article:

Broome, S.A. (1989). "The Magic Kids: A Strategy to Build Self-Esteem and Change Attitudes Toward the Handicapped." Paper presented at the Annual Convention of the Council for Exceptional Children (67th, San Francisco, CA, April 3-7, 1989).

Broome, S.A. (1995). "Magic in the Classroom." *Beyond Behavior.*

My Magic Kids in Macon will always be remembered as my first Magic Kids. They hold a special place in my heart.

Is Golf Really a Gentleman's Sport?

———◆———

Is golf really a gentleman's sport? I wonder. When I was little, my mom loved to play golf. Mom and Dad taught me how to play. Of course, all of us started with putt putt or miniature golf during our family vacations to Myrtle Beach. It was a big deal to get a hole in one. Of course, we were taught to keep the right score and not cheat. That was tough sometimes. We loved miniature golf with all the animated characters. But my folks taught me to play real golf and I thought that was so cool. My mom's favorite was Par 3. The distance to the hole was shorter. Mom played like a champ and was very competitive. One time, she got a birdie, a super great shot in golf. No, she really hit a live bird in flight. Then there was the time when someone on the other hole hit a ball from the tee that hit me hard in the leg. You cannot imagine that really, if you have never been hit with a golf ball. It is a special experience. A big knot came up on my leg, but I did get a free coke. That is what they gave me to put on my leg for the swelling and the folks at the golf shop made a big deal out of it. To me, the storyteller, this just gave me a story to tell. To this day, I have a score card where I got a hole in one and am supposed to get a free game. Do they still honor that after 30 years? I doubt it but I just still love to look at that scorecard.

My brother went to college at the University of North Carolina at Chapel Hill. He was eight years older so that means that I was only about 11. I was skinny; my brother was not. He did all the skinny jokes. He said that if I had a run in my pantyhose, I would fall out. He said that I would have to dance around in the shower to get wet. And because I was a big talker, he said that I was just a mouth on a backbone! Chapel Hill was a great place for the parents and me to visit. This of course gave Mom an excuse to find a golf course and work in a game of golf. Learning to play that young did help me learn to like the game of golf. It can be a lifetime sport, both the short and the long game.

When I met Paul, I told him about my love of golf. That was something that we could enjoy together. One day, in Macon, we were playing, and Paul hit his golf ball. A big old shank off the tee and the ball flew into a metal shed like an airplane hangar with big double doors. You could hear that golf ball going "ping, ping" all over that metal shed. The employees ran out of the shed and hit the dirt like a hand grenade had gone off in the building. Well, the pro came over and proceeded to give ME a golf lesson. Talk about making an assumption. He just assumed that little Annie Mae made that bad shot. I just let him have at it and took my free lesson in stride, never revealing that Paul hit that wicked ball. (Gentleman' sport?) Paul did not own up to it either.

Oh, balls to the left, balls to the right, but I have to say I was pretty good until we got to the water hole. Normally, I had no problem hitting the ball a nice distance off the tee, but that pond or lake was like a magnet to me. I gave the golf course a whole lot of golf balls if I could not fish the ball out. Then if I did, I would often be in the sand trap. Well, Paul may not have been a gentleman when he did not own his bad shot, but I was sure no lady with all the cussing that I did when my ball went in the lake. I would hop around and do the Fuck Fuck chorus. That would always crush my usually good game too.

We would regale our friends with our funny golf stories. William was a good, avid golf player. He and Anne said, "Let's go play." We went out to the municipal golf course where you could play for a minimal price. It was Bowden Golf Course, which opened in 1940 and is still there. Here went the four of us. Oh, you are visualizing us in polo shirts with little spikes on our shoes, a golf cart full of beer…well let me just say no to every bit of that. We had on shorts, t shirts, tennis shoes and were carrying our few meager clubs as we walked the course. Poor Anne had never played. She got off to a rough start, but that chick doesn't give up. She was not cussing and carrying on like crazy Annie Mae. We hung in there. Poor William. Paul discovered that he could psych William out. William would be at the tee ready to hit the ball. Paul would say, "William, do you blink when you hit the ball?" William, of course, would balk. The daylight was fading to dark. Paul hit a nice ball that was on the fairway. William hit a bad ball and thought he was sneaking and put another one out. He was kind of sliding the ball down his leg. He was not a gentleman. Paul was right there behind William, but William did not know it until Paul tapped him on the shoulder; *busted William*, caught literally in the act of cheating. Paul did his little bit of evil golf also. When no one was looking, we thought that Paul had buried William's ball. William would look all over for the golf ball, and then there he went, trying to take out another one. It turned out that there was a wet area that was like quicksand. Paul hit his ball, and it, too, disappeared. While he was looking for his ball, he found 12 other balls that had gone into the muddy area. Needless to say, it was a long, sweaty day.

Now, you know how we teachers can smell a great conference a mile away. I got selected to go to a conference in Pinehurst, North Carolina. Why that is the golfing capital of North Carolina? It is the anchor site for the US Open. It is the cradle of American golf, where it has been played for 125 years. Does it just have 18 holes like Bowden? No, it has nine golf courses, all with different designs (information taken from Pinehurst website). Now, I was able to meet new people who were selected for the conference. Tabitha, a PE teacher that I had never met, was to be my roommate. We rode with Calvin, an art teacher, and the golf coach for a prestigious high school. He even has a RING, meaning that one of his teams won a state championship. Impressive. When we arrived and went to check in, the lobby was chock full of people trying to check in. We nudged our way up to the front. The boss was watching to make sure that we were behaving. I finally got to the front desk only to find out that they were overbooked but had put us in a suite. What a suite, I SCREAMED out loud right there in that full lobby.

Now, the issue was that there was only one bed and I said, "Why, I just met her, I can't sleep with her."

"Well, honey, it is a large suite, and we can bring up a bed."

Tabitha said, "Sa-weet, a suite."

I yelled, "SWEET."

The boss was aghast. Why, everyone was looking at us making a spectacle. I did not care. I was SO happy. Today is my day. We had one of the Donald Ross suites. Donald Ross was the famous person who had designed the golf courses. That suite was the party capital for all 18 of us during the whole trip. Why, my suite had a foyer and artwork, and a big TV, recliners, and a bar!!!!!!!!!!! The balcony was huge with a view of the golf courses.

Calvin had been to Pinehurst many times since he played golf regularly. Calvin decided that we should all go out bar hopping that night. There was even a shuttle that would take us to town to the bars and restaurants. There we went, all 18 of us. Calvin took us to a bar where you could chip a ball into the fireplace. I know that sounds ridiculous. But yes, it was set up so you could tee up a ball, yes right there in the bar restaurant, into the fireplace. We bellied up to the bar and I got a Guinness. We were all getting beers. Well, Calvin just got a bar stool and watched us fools. Tabitha, of course, shot the ball right into the fireplace. Others did too. Then it was my turn. My mojo was just not there that night. I guess I had used up all my rightful karma getting the lucky suite. A lady was sitting nearby, and I almost hit her. One of my balls flew into the restaurant, there it went, bounce, bounce, bounce. At that point, a man came over from the bar and offered to give me a golf lesson. "What is your name?"

"Annie Mae." Even though I was happily married to Paul, I loved to flirt. I always say that being on a diet does not mean that you cannot read a menu. Paul also liked it when men flirted with me. It made him feel good to have a wife who other men found attractive. Well, the man from the bar got behind me and had his arms over my arms and next thing I knew he had his hand on my ass— literally, sure he was trying to help me hit the ball. Every time, he had me in a clutch with his hand on my ass.

My loyal roommate, that I had just met, said, "I see that hand on her ass. Get your hand off her ass." Calvin was looking and shaking his head.

Then another man said, "My turn, let me help her."

Wow, did I say it was my lucky day. I had not had that much contact sex in quite a while. I was yelling, "I love this place," when Calvin said, "Annie Mae, I believe it is time to go." Calvin was not a fan of that much flirtation.

The next day, I was in class, being diligent and taking copious notes. Calvin was supposed to be helping the boss get ready for her presentation. Next thing, I knew, someone asked Calvin to go look at the golf courses. He saw all the golf courses, played golf and, oh Hell, we all got a tour of the golf courses. That was such a great trip that I bought a martini glass that is on top of a glass golf ball. It is so damn cute and says Pinehurst. I stayed in the Donald Ross suite, got to go out and drink beer with great new friends, had a man's hand on my ass, and shot a golf ball into the fireplace. Is there more to life than this? But then I say again, "is golf a gentleman's sport?"

Well, taking this golf memoir back to Macon, Paul was asked by the law school to help host a conference for local lawyers that included a golf tournament. He got paid to be the videographer for the conference sessions. Mel, one of Paul law school buddies and I got hired to be caterers for the conference and for the golf tournament.

There was a ton of food and kegs of beer. We were so glad to get paid. Holy Cow. Then once the conference ended and we cleaned up we got to take the leftover food and a keg of beer. Party time in the Bell front yard. We set up the keg and the food right there in front of the apartments and got lawn chairs. We were all eating and drinking and making merry. Paul felt that Mel was being just a little too happy with me (guess he could only handle a little flirtation after all) and he folded Mel up in his lawn chair. This was, yet again, another story that stemmed from the age-old game of golf. It may not be a gentleman's sport all the time, but it sure brings on a lot of fun.

The Rabbit is Rich

———•———

If you read *Sick and Twisted in Savannah*, you will know about the summer internship that Paul did in Savannah the summer prior to his graduation from Mercer Law School. He had done an internship for my dad, who was an attorney in Cherryville, but we both felt that it was time to experience something a little different from a family practice and maybe something that would lead to a future job in Georgia practicing law. We knew that he would have to take some time to study for the North Carolina Bar Exam prior to being eligible for a job in North Carolina. There is a book called Martindale and Hubble. It lists lawyers from all over the country. I took that book and literally sent out 200 requests for an internship in Georgia. Bingo, he got an internship in Savannah. We were thrilled. Of course, I remained in Macon with a summer job teaching Intro to Special Ed at Armstrong College and teaching students in a special summer program.

Paul was able to rent an apartment in an antebellum house in what was called a "transitional neighborhood."

That was code for trying to gentrify a ghetto. It had a clawfoot tub in the turret. You could take your bubble bath and look over the city of Savannah. Super, fucking cool I am telling you. This is where we met his neighbor Buck who we later introduced to Lois, the neighbor in Macon, who saw our Peeping Tom. I was "Best Man" in their wedding. This was also the neighborhood where I was robbed at the laundromat. I would visit Paul each weekend and we would ride out to Tybee Beach on the motorcycle, and we had a ball. When we moved to Macon, we had to sell Paul's car. A motorcycle was much cheaper to run and fun to boot. WHOOOH WEE that was the time that we were making love in the ocean and a wave took Paul's bathing suit. Naked lawyer alert. You may just need to read *Sick and Twisted in Savannah.*

Anyway, since I was going to be alone while Paul was in Savannah, William, Anne, Vergie, Tim, everyone was worried about poor little Annie Mae. I had never lived alone and don't always have the best judgment or quick thinking in a crisis of any kind. Paul and William said there should be a code word so that if William called me each night, I could say the code word and he would know that I was OK. The code word was "the rabbit is rich." Every night, literally, he called me, and I said, "The rabbit is rich." All was good. I really liked my two jobs. Intro to Special Ed had a great group of folks. At the end of that session, they totally surprised the dickens out of me. I had told them about my Magic Kids when I taught the lesson on Behavior Disorders. For my parting gift, they gave me a music box with a rabbit that came out of the magic hat on top. I was thrilled and cried a proverbial river. I am looking at it right now after all these years. My other job was teaching middle and high school students in a technical school who were considered at risk for dropping out. A friend of a friend offered me the job and I snapped it up. He was an amateur magician and came to my class to give my students pointers before our magic show and he thought I would be a good fit for this summer job. I taught them reading and math skills and we also did a class meeting each day and they wrote in their journals. The journals were great for building relationships because we could write back and forth to each other every day. My classroom was on a hall with other classrooms. Well, the "gentleman" NOT, next to me was the sheet metal instructor. Well, you know, as Paul often says, I am no Sherlock Holmes and get a little lost in the details. I thought he was wearing a Star of David around his neck. He was never friendly and did not even really speak to me. That is super tough on a southern gal, so I tried to strike up a conversation with him one morning before school. I told him that I had best friends in North Carolina who were Jewish and that I had the privilege of being involved in Seder and other Jewish celebrations. He growled at me. I was like seriously. He stomped away. Maybe his tattoos and piercings should have tipped me off. Anyway, when I asked the boss, he said, "Oh, for Hell's sake, Annie Mae. He is not wearing a Star of David. He is wearing a Pentagram. He is a Warlock and has a coven of witches and is all about the occult. Stay away from him."

"Well, slap my face and call me Porky, no wonder he was so pissed off. Damn, a real live Warlock right next door. That is creepy cool."

Well, in addition to not warning me about the sheet metal instructor, the boss forgot to tell me that he did "fire drills" on Friday afternoon once the kids were gone. That was just his excuse for everyone to leave the building early on Fridays. Man, that first Friday when that alarm was blaring, you talk about running. "Fucking feet, don't fail me now." I ran out of that vocational building like a scalded dog. The boss was laughing but it was not a damn bit funny. I had no purse, no keys, and no cake or little Krystals that I was taking to Paul. Little Krystals are the small burgers sold at the Krystal Restaurant. He did let me back in to get my stuff, but he was like, "Girl please, it is Friday and you are making me late for day drinking."

I would be back in Macon for work on Mondays. You have heard me talk about Buffy, my nanny, my soulmate, my other mother, my lifeline. Well, she decided to come visit me in Macon. She came down on the bus. Well, I was worried sick about her. What if something happened to my Big Mama? I called every stop between Gastonia, North Carolina, and Macon, Georgia, to be sure that my Buffy was still on the right bus. When she finally arrived, she was happy and had made a lot of friends on the bus. "Girl what is wrong with you calling at every stop like I don't have sense enough to ride the bus? You know you are the only white child I ever beat. I think I need to get the giant can of Butt Whip out right now and beat your ass as long as your ass lasts." Oh, all those people on the bus were laughing hysterically at me and Buffy.

Well, we had a ball. She could rest during the day while I worked and we could go out or eat in at night. We cooked all kinds of good food. Well, my buddy from work, Hut, had a party at her house in honor of Buffy's visit. All the gang was there and brought food and booze. Buffy and I got sassy dressed and were greeted warmly upon arrival at Huts. We were getting pretty tanked. Hut, Deaconess, Sassy, Joseph, a whole bunch of us were just hanging out in the kitchen. Everybody was looking at Joseph and Buffy. Joseph was one of my close work buddies. Just look at those two. Joseph was all hugged up with Buffy and she kept calling him her little pork tenderloin. That had the crew all torn up. Joseph kept hugging her a little closer each time she said, "my little pork tenderloin" till finally Buffy pinches Joseph's cheek and says to Joseph. "Now, Little Pork Tenderloin, don't start something tonight that you can't finish." Well, that really got The Group going. We all fell out. You should have seen Joseph. The little pork tenderloin was speechless.

Now, I got home from work one day anticipating the great southern food Buffy and I were going to cook up for dinner. I am so lucky that Buffy taught me to cook. She was the greatest cook. At one time in Cherryville, Buffy was the cook for Carolina Freight. That was a major national trucking company housed in my hometown.

People would pile in that cafeteria on Sundays to get the best fried chicken and mac and cheese on the planet. Well, I entered the apartment with my growling stomach only to find no Buffy. Buffy, "Big Mama." She was not there. I went to the various neighbors until I got to Miss Myrtle's and she said that she thought Buffy left with Keith. "With Keith? Bloody Hell. He was the crazy, wild neighbor who was into all sorts of shenanigans. Oh Hell, not Keith taking my Buffy up in a plane. I mean a very small plane, a two-seater. I did not think there was enough liquor on the planet to get Buffy in one of those planes and especially with Keith as the pilot. Lord have mercy on us all, dear Jesus. All I could do was pray. If he has done killed my Big Mama, I will never be able to live without her and I could never go back to Cherryville without her. Oh, my God, what to do, what to do? I felt so helpless. I was running and screaming and did not even know what to do next. When, they showed up, laughing and talking about what a great time they had. Well, I hit the ceiling. "You motherfuckers, you have scared the Hell out of me and scared me into my next life." Buffy was saying she had the best time. They flew all over Macon.

"Why, Keith just needed some of those flight hours and we flew to Augusta."

"It was so beautiful."

Keith said that they had so much fun. "I love Buffy. She is even way more fun than you."

That Friday, I came home with a bag of little burgers from Krystals. Buffy had made all manner of good food. There was ham, tater salad, and mac and cheese to take to Savannah. We packed the car and took off Buffy and me. We got to the apartment and Paul and Dawn and Jimmy were there too. To this day, I do not know how we all fit in there. We did not have furniture. We just had air mattresses but somehow, we made it work. Oh my goodness, we took Buffy down to River Street. Buffy tried to pick up our favorite policeman who was out in front of Spanky's, a popular restaurant, and had us our traditional gift of a chicken finger basket. She thought she had found another cute little pork tenderloin. We hustled her along. We went all over River Street eating and drinking and showing Buffy the sights. It was just great. Then here we go back to Macon on Sunday. I had to get her on that bus on Monday. I decided to put on my big girl panties and not worry about Buffy on the bus. I guess I got the wrong panties because there I was again taking breaks from work and calling every bus stop. She made it home safely. It was a wonderful week to remember.

I decided one night that it was time to go visit Keith and Laura. That way I could fuss at him again just a little bit about taking to the friendly skies with my Buffy. Keith and Laura said that they had a little treat for me. They had Alice B. Toklas brownies, that meant they were chocolate brownies laced with pot. I had never had one before. We each ate that first brownie, and it was so good. We sat at the kitchen table playing games and drinking beer. I could not believe that a brownie could be so good and make one feel so good. Well, if one brownie was good, what would two be like? I was feeling mighty fine. Could two be twice as good? I don't know about twice as good, but I was twice as high, high as a Georgia pine. I don't even remember how I got down the steps from their apartment. I felt like it must have been hours. I crawled across the gravel driveway on my hands and knees. What a hot, scratched up mess I was. I could not stand up. I could not walk. Finally, I did rise up and somehow knee walk the stairs up into my apartment. I do remember turning on the TV and thinking it was alive. I was terrified and crazed. I thought that all those characters were coming out of the TV. Man oh man. Then I heard the phone ringing. It was William. He said, hi Annie Mae. I said nothing. Annie Mae, where is the rabbit? I could barely talk and grunted "what rabbit?" "Annie Mae, does the rabbit have any money?" Again, I grunted, "what rabbit? OK, I am on my way. Boy, was William surprised when he arrived. He thought he might find me robbed or raped or both. But no, he found me lying on the floor, wasted. What the Hell has happened to you? Oh, my Lord, what will Paul think. He was not one to do drugs or be all crazy acting especially with work the next day. Paul will not be happy. NO shit! Well, let me just say, oh, what a night. I will give you a tip. If one brownie is good, just go with that and be happy. That two is twice as good just does not work. You might find yourself high as a Georgia Pine, all scratched up, bruised and acting crazy, and you might not even remember that "the rabbit is rich."

Life Can be a Beach

The boys were having a little break from law school and summer internships. Tina Dawn was going to spend some summertime with her dad in Cherryville, so Paul and I decided to go camping at the beach. We had some past good times prior to law school camping at Huntington Beach State Park in South Carolina. It is a five-star campground in Georgetown County. It was near the Atalaya castle, the picturesque Moorish winter home of Archer and Anna Hyatt Huntington (well it is a castle to me) and Brookgreen Gardens. The gardens have beautiful sculptures done by Anna Hyatt Huntington. The state park has saltmarsh walkways, a lake with gators, and three miles of undeveloped beach. We met friendly people there. It is a certain type of person that is comfortable camping.

One year, we met a couple from Coal Run, Idaho. They were millionaires. Everybody in their town struck oil but even wealthy, this couple camped here every year. You would never have known they had money, but the story was interesting. They said that each member of this small town gathered at the post office each week to get their checks and see how much money they were making. Well, our story that year was not quite as grand. We were living in Cherryville, thankfully, close to Mom and Dad. Paul and I got off work on a Friday for the whole summer free and took off like our pants were on fire toward our vacation at the campground. He was a social worker for the schools, and I was a teacher, and we had the whole summer off. Free as birds, without a care in the crazy world of work. Wow, that was until Mom called and said that I forgot to put our payroll check in the bank prior to leaving and that all our checks *were bouncing around the county like rubber balls. Living in a small town really has its advantages. The bank called Mom to let her know that we were overdrawn.* I'm so glad Mom had a key to our house and could get our check and make the deposit. Whew! Close one!

While we were in Macon and William and Paul were in law school, we decided to take a summer beach trip. This summer trip involved Paul and I getting to the Huntington Beach State Campground and locating a great space to set up our tent and screen house. I like a strategic location not far from the bath house. I get lost everywhere and being lost in the night going to the potty is not fun, especially with me, who seems to need to pee every hour. We determined, prior to leaving Macon, that William would join us at some point. My parents were also coming and staying in a motel in North Myrtle Beach.

Prior to the arrival of our guests, we decided to have a night out at the disco. Oh yeah, disco was big back then in the 80's and even camping, I had to get myself ready for disco night. I had on a cute top, my spandex wrap skirt and dancing heels. No panties, of course. Wild and Free on disco night. Why, Hell, I even had a butane curling iron. I decided to be SO ready for a romantic and sexy night out that I had my Ben Wah Balls in a Velvet Box. They were a saucy gift from my sexy husband. I thought I knew how to use them even though they did not come with instructions. Don't disparage me. We did not have YouTube or the internet for every question one might have. I went into the bath house, while Paul was waiting for me right outside, and put those gold balls right into my pussy. They were rolling around and tapping up in there. I came sashaying out trying to really evoke the mood for the night when much to my utter surprise, *those damn gold balls rolled right out of my hoo hoo onto the dirt path and rolled down the hill with me chasing them.* Not exactly the mood I wanted to evoke on our night out. Paul should still be laughing. It was a sight to behold.

We continued to the disco and had a wonderful night out partying and in the tent partying upon return. William arrived the next day and so did my parents. My parents were so great. They took us out to eat at a nice restaurant and paid for the meal for all of us. As well as I remember, we slept well and got up to start our fishing day. William commented on my gold lame bathing suit and was that really fishing attire. It was for me. I liked to fish and sun at the same time. We were in the ocean with our baited hooks, when William screamed and ran out of the water. Something had touched him in the ocean. Paul and I were just about laughing too hard to fish. We had a great day and caught some whiting to grill for dinner. We had vegetables from a local produce stand. That along with the grilled fish would be a superb dinner for us. We cleaned the fish and saved the fish heads to use to bait for crabs the next day. We said that we loved living by the tides. William was all about living by the tides too until he bit into the fish. "These fish have bones!"

"Well, yes, they do. We have not been able to learn to catch them filleted."

The crabs the next day were excellent, and we surf fished in the ocean again also. We decided that before William returned to Macon, we should go out fishing in a boat. I was super excited about the prospect. Paul and I had not done that before. William fished a lot with his buddies and assured us it would be a great time.

Early the next morning, William, Paul, and I went to the docks and rented a small skiff. We had our fishing gear, sunscreen, beer, and snacks and set off through the marsh. The tides and motor were carrying us nicely out and we put our hooks in the water. It got hot out there fishing, so every little while we would take off out to another area to fish and let the winds cool us off. We were having so much fun telling stories and just enjoying a day out with the fish. I don't even remember what or how many we caught. It was just damn good fun and what a great way to spend William's last day of vacation with us before he headed back to Macon. We began to be low on beer and the sun was beginning to set and we figured we better head back inland. We started motoring back and the tide was running out and everything looked different. We turned a few places and then realized that we did not know where we were.

That is when I remembered another fishing trip that William took while we were living in Macon. He and some of his Macon buddies went duck hunting one weekend down the Ogeechee River, near Annette, Georgia. They were drinking and having a ball getting ducks left and right. There again, when their motor died, they realized they were lost on the river. They just floated along and began to have to throw ducks out of the boat. They were drifting and it was getting dark. They spotted a shelter and took the boat there and got out for the night. They still had beer and some snacks and had an OK night in the shelter. The next day, they went out again and began, yet again, to drift aimlessly along, figuring that sooner or later someone would spot them and assist. Little did they know that when they did not come home the next day, literally (not just the expression) Hell and half of Georgia was looking for them. Anne, Paul, and I were frantic back in Macon and assumed that they had drowned. There were crews out on the river looking for them and a helicopter flying over. They were spotted and returned to safety only to realize that they were all over the news as "lost duck hunters." We all had many laughs over that crazy, misspent adventure with those fools not even knowing they were infamous.

So, OK, I began to rib William about his prowess as a hunter and fisherman when Paul took over and began to motor us back toward the docks. Paul has a great sense of direction and was talking about reading the tides and shit and sure enough we did make it in before dark. Even with the little bit of fear gnawing at my gut, it was still a great day. It was hard to say bye to William.

Paul and I continued to swim, fish, eat and drink our merry way through the rest of our beach trip. It was an awesome time. Life really can be a beach!

There Goes a Meatball

It was time for final exams. William and Paul were so focused on doing well on those exams. So focused and dedicated that they decided to go out and drink copious amounts of booze. Drink, they did. Paul swears to this day that one of the bartenders was trying to kill them. He kept serving them Tequila long, long after they should have been cut off and the place was closed. They went down memory lane, going to all our favorite bars from our time in Macon. The bars back in those days could do Happy Hour, Hungry Hour with appetizers and 2 for one or 3 for one drinks. The bar scene there in the 80s was alive and well. Paul and I were used to Cherryville where the bar scene was buying a six pack and taking it to the house. The boys had a really good time from what I heard. They even tried to break up a fight. Someone, they said, was picking on a gay guy. Don't know if they were preventing the fight, in the fight, who knows? Poor guy, they said they gave him a ride home and that is scarier to me than the beatings. The events of that night are a little sketchy.

I had to work the next day, so I was home in bed asleep. This chick had to hunker down and go night

night. At some point during the night, Paul thought he was creeping quietly into the house not to wake up Tina Dawn and me. He was all over the place, stumbling and staggering into things. He came into the bedroom and knocked the lamp to the floor. I think he was going to try to get into the bed when he began to barf. I mean puke his guts out. But I tell you, it was the weirdest thing. He was not retching or gagging or anything like that. His mouth was open, and the vomit was flowing out like a fountain. It was flowing onto the bed. I was trying to pretend I was asleep so that I would not have to deal with it. But then, he said, "look there goes a meatball, oh look another meatball, and now I think that is a cocktail weenie."

I swear, I could not stop laughing. That was the damn, craziest, funniest thing I had seen in a long time. I bolted upright in the bed because I had to laugh so hard. There he was with his flowing fountain talking about food coming up whole. What does one do with that, I ask? I don't know how he made it through the night.

The boys somehow did pass their finals. They got to take the Georgia Bar exam early prior to graduation. That was neat. If they passed, they were job ready. They went to a hotel bar in Macon where someone came in carrying the names from a newspaper. This was all such an exciting time in our lives. We had left Cherryville and struggled a bit along the way to get to this point. I had trouble containing my pride. I was so proud of Paul. He had done so well. During law school, he was part of the

Moot Court Team and part of the Trial Practice Team. His professor took the teams to Florida to compete. Georgia got a van and Paul, Georgia, Natty, Burt and the Professor took to the road. Secretly, I knew that the professor had a crush on Paul. We had been invited to her house for a party and she just looked at him like she could eat him up. It was all OK and the team came in second in the competition, and they arrived home safely. While in law school, Tim made Law Review which is a huge honor. We were all proud of our husbands and the husbands were proud of their wives. We had all learned a lot in those three years.

Paul did not want to make a big deal out of graduation from Mercer Law School. What? What? I was damn determined to make a huge deal out of it and invited the whole famdamily, my mom, dad, brother, his wife, their three kids, Paul's parents, his sister, Dawn, and her boyfriend, Jimmy. They all got motel rooms, and we got food for pick- ups and desserts. I was thrilled for all of them to be there with us. There were two ceremonies: the graduation at the Coliseum and a Hooding Ceremony. The Hooding Ceremony was separate and in a garden area. It was so nice and even had a good speaker. Even Tina Dawn and the cousins were impressed. Then it was time for the graduation ceremony across town. I do not know how I ended up being the one in the car with Paul's parents, but we just rode around. Finally, his dad said, "You don't know how to get to the Coliseum do you?" "You have lived here for three years and don't know where the Coliseum is." Well, no. Yes, you know, we got there after his name had been called. They did not get to see their son get his law school diploma. Paul's parents, needless to say, were not happy with me. There were many times that they were not happy with me, but this just put the proverbial nail in my coffin. But not to worry. We all went to Paul's favorite restaurant with a huge Asian menu and had a superb meal with the parents footing the bill. My mom made sure that I got a present, gold and diamond hoop earrings. She knew from her own life experience what it was like to be the law spouse and she was proud of me too. We went to the motel where all the famdamily were staying and hung out at the pool. We felt that this time was so special. We were so proud of Tim, William, Paul, Natty, Burt and Georgia and the whole crew for persevering and getting ready to move on to the next chapter with new jobs. Paul knew that he had a job in a Savannah law firm, and I knew that I would be teaching there. When I went in to tell my boss that I was leaving Macon. He said that I was leaving the best job I would ever have in my life. Oh, no, thinking about leaving Hut, Deaconess, Sassy, Joseph, Anne, Vergie, and Miss Myrtle, etc., etc., etc. I believed him and cried a river. I did not want anyone to have my job. What fools were they? They let me be on the interview team. I did not want it to be a fun, sassy person so we hired a nun. No lie. Macon gave me a great retirement party. The theme was "A Saint you Ain't but a Star You Are." That was so perfect. All good things must come to an end. This was an end and a beginning and look out for the next meatball

Epilogue 2024

Did the Mischief Makers live happily ever after? They left Savannah, Georgia, after only two years to return home to Cherryville to look after their parents. Annie Mae is still working in education and having a ball!

Tina Dawn is married with a daughter and took cheerleading to a whole new level in sales.

William and Anne: Anne has retired as an elementary school principal and William is still practicing law in Georgia.

Tim and Vergie: Tim and Vergie both retired from successful careers in law and landscape architecture to move home to look after their parents, children, and grandchildren.

Dawn and Jimmy: Dawn has retired from her job as a Speech Language Pathologist and Jimmy passed away recently. We all really miss Jimmy and his mischief.

Natty, Burt, Mel, and Georgia all became successful attorneys. Burt has passed away and he is truly missed by our crew.

Buffy and "Hut" are both deceased, but their legacies live on. Deaconess, Joseph, and Sassy are alive and well still partying even without Buffy and "Hut."

The Mischief Makers still get together and love to remember that golden time in their lives when they were pursuing their futures and having fun developing lifelong friendships.

Meet the Author

———◆———

Sadie Allran Broome has been a public-school educator, teaching students with disabilities, for over forty years. During that time, she has been "Teacher of the Year" in Gaston County, North Carolina and in Bibb County, Georgia.

Sadie has co-authored three books on teaching character in the elementary, middle and teenage years. She was a Christa McAuliffe Fellow and Non-Teaching Educator of the Year in Gaston County Schools. Her works have been published in two journals and she recently collaborated with an educator in the United Kingdom on a research article. Sadie was recipient of the Cardinal Award and the Order of the Long Leaf Pine Award in the state of North Carolina.

Sadie has published an adult memoir, *Sick and Twisted in Savannah; the Victory Street Irregulars*.

She is at home in Cherryville, North Carolina. She is married to Dennis and is a proud mother and grandmother. She enjoys playing the flute, writing and traveling. Her passions are spending time with her family, friends and teaching.

www.ingramcontent.com/pod-product-compliance
Lightning Source LLC
LaVergne TN
LVHW011838060526
838200LV00054B/4089